AFRICAN WRITERS SERIES
Editorial Adviser . Chinua Achebe

32
Kinsman and Foreman

AFRICAN WRITERS SERIES

Kinsman and Foreman

T. M. ALUKO

HEINEMANN
LONDON IBADAN NAIROBI

Heinemann Educational Books Ltd
48 Charles Street, London W1X 8AH
PMB 5205, Ibadan · POB 25080, Nairobi
EDINBURGH   MELBOURNE   TORONTO
AUCKLAND   HONG KONG   SINGAPORE

SBN 435 90032 3

Printed in Malta by
St Paul's Press Ltd

One

———◇———

As soon as he entered the long parlour a spontaneous outburst of wailing greeted Titus from the other end. The voices were mostly female, chanting different messages to the departed one:

'You must wait for me at heaven's gate, brother mine!'

'Wretched, wretched me!'

'My world is in ruins, my husband in heaven!'

Titus, poor boy, knew what it was all about. These relatives were, for the umpteenth time, crying in chorus over the death of his father, who had died nineteen months before. Titus recollected how he had nearly gone mad with grief the day he received the cable in London telling him that his father had died – how he had cried for days on end in his digs. He recollected, also, how he had ridden aimlessly on buses and in the Underground trying to puzzle out how he was going to complete his studies now that the source of his money had suddenly dried up. And he recollected that, the evening before, this same crowd that had gathered so happily to welcome him back from England had also suddenly started their mass wailing.

He knew it was the custom. He knew that whenever any member of the family arrives back from a distant place, the clan gathers together and wails together over the loss of this or that dear one who had died whilst the new arrival was absent.

The wailing crowd into which he was now being led by his mother, who carried a clay lamp burning palm oil, were the relatives from both sides of the extended family. They had assembled at dawn after the day of his arrival to welcome him and to demonstrate once more their grief at the death of his father, their kinsman.

Besides the lamp which his mother carried, there were two other lamps placed in recesses in the mud wall. There was also a hurricane-lamp at the foot of a chair on which sat a man whom Titus could not immediately recognize. The truth was that he could not recognize anyone or anything immediately. The combined effect of all four lamps amounted to little in terms of illumination and his eyes had not yet adjusted themselves to the change from the deeper darkness outside. Someone, still wailing, guided him to a chair next to the one near the hurricane lantern. He noticed that his mother proceeded to take her seat on a mud dais. She joined the others, who made room for her, in the mass wailing. He himself was not crying.

'Enough! It is enough!' the man on the chair next to him cried in a voice of authority. He at once recognized the voice to be that of his great-uncle Joel. He watched him rise, take a few steps and clap his hands. The crying subsided.

'This wailing must stop,' the old man cried. 'I repeat: this crying must stop. I have come this morning to welcome my child Titus. I have not come to bury my nephew Samuel all over again. That most painful duty I have performed already – and finished with. It was the tragedy of my life that I should live to see the end of the son of my brother. Silence, silence,' he roared as one

2

female voice resumed sobbing. 'If there is anyone here who is not able to control her emotions let her go out of here – now. Let her leave us to perform the important business before us. Who wanted all you women here, anyway?'

He adjusted the velvet wrapper and slung the sleeve high up across his left shoulder. He took three short steps to the mud dais where the women sat.

'I salute you all for your great courage,' he said. 'I salute you all. Titus, the son of the son of my brother has come back from the white man's country. He sits here with us. He has come back to dry the tears of all of us. That is why we must welcome him with gladness, and not greet him with more tears.'

There was another round of wailing which Pa Joel stopped fiercely, after allowing it to flourish for some time. Then an old woman spoke in a faltering voice, 'Is it true that Titus has come back? Come to me, my child.'

Titus recognized his great-aunt, the younger sister of Pa Joel. He saw that old age had affected her rather badly. He rose, took a few short steps to the dais, and knelt before the old woman. He held her shrivelled left hand in his right. She herself lifted her right hand to his head and ran her shrivelled fingers through the forest of hair. She was full of emotion.

'Titus, my child, you have come back to me. You have come back from the country of the white man. And I thank God that the white man has allowed you to come back to me, Titus . . . Titus, when you were about to go on the great journey, this was where you sat next to me. On this same mat . . . at dawn, like this. When Pastor came, and we sang songs. And Pastor read prayers from the Book . . .'

Titus's eyes were now quite adjusted to the poor light.

He noticed that his great-aunt wore no blouse and that her loin-cloth was wrapped round her waist. It could not give her much protection from the cold. She continued,

'You know I prayed for you then, Titus. I told you that you would go safely and you would return safely – the hand never meets with disaster in its regular journeys to and from the mouth during a meal . . . and I told you one other thing, Titus, while you sat near me, on this same dais. I told you that you would come back to find me still alive . . . I am still alive . . . But . . . but the wicked people of Ibala . . . they have . . . ' Here her voice trailed off into inaudibility. The crowd started another round of crying.

The old man Joel again called for silence. He gave the impression that he thought that he had allowed his sister enough time in which to indulge her harmless doting. He said,

'We are all here, both sides of the family. I want you all to listen patiently to the words of my mouth. I am an old man, and I must not speak too long. That is why I want you to listen to the few words I am going to say now. This child that has come back to us from the country of the white man is going to hold the post of a white man in Government work. There is no other African who knows the work as well as he does. That is why he is going to be given the post of a white man. It is a very delicate and dangerous thing for a young man to be holding such a very high post. We must see to it that he is properly armed. And this is the reason why I am here this morning, to hand my child Titus to his kinsman Simeon.'

He stopped for a little while. He re-adjusted the cloth over his shoulder. A mouthful of saliva slid down his ancient throat.

'Simeon and Titus are one,' he went on. 'But for the

4

White Man that has come to confuse the world, is Simeon not entitled to inherit Deborah the mother of Titus after her husband Samuel died? Are my words not true?' he asked rebukingly in the direction of one of the women that had giggled at the suggestion of Simeon taking over Deborah. 'Why cannot Simeon take over Deborah after her husband died, I ask? Is she past child-bearing? I warn you women never again to distract my attention when I am saying very important words from my mouth.' He was quite annoyed; they all saw it. The erring woman looked genuinely penitent.

'In the whole of Ibala there is no one in the P.W.D. that knows the work as well as Simeon,' he continued. 'He has been in the work since he was a child. When many years ago he ran away from the farm to go to school his father was very cross. He reported him to me but I advised him to let the boy go to school if that was what he wanted and if he could stand the flogging there. I told your father, Simeon, that the world was turning to the world of the white man and therefore no one must force his child to stay on the farm if he did not wish to be a farmer. That was what I told your father; I remember it well. And when you ran away from school to join Government work I advised your father not to be annoyed over it. Pastor had wanted you to be a teacher . . . But do we all not now see the work of God? Have you not become the most important man in Government work here in Ibala? Are we not very happy about this?'

One woman intoned: 'Glory be to God. Hallelujah.'

Joel gulped another mouthful of saliva down his throat.

Deborah adjusted the wick of the lamp she held in her hand. The woman nearest one of the two lamps in the recesses in the wall took the cue from her and proceeded to adjust the wick in the oil in the other lamp. There was a marked increase of light in the long room. Old Joel continued,

'We are this morning handing Titus, our son, to Simeon his father, to look after him in Government work. And when I call Titus the son of Simeon don't think that I'm saying the words of a doting old man. Don't think that I am saying that Titus was in fact fathered by Simeon. No, not so. But even if Simeon had an illicit affair with Deborah the wife of his Cousin Samuel would that be unheard of in the land?' He looked round the group. Deborah adjusted the wick in the oil in the lamp, embarrassed by the words of the old man.

Joel then took three steps to where Titus was sitting. He held his left hand and dragged him up. Titus followed the old man to where Simeon sat, smoking a cigarette. 'Simeon, this is Titus the son of your kinsman Samuel, now gone to heaven. I hand him to you this day as your own son. You are to direct his going out and his coming in in the P.W.D. You know all the intricacies of Government work. Titus has only the book knowledge of Government work; he does not know the other side. You know it. If the railway train runs non-stop for a hundred years, will it not always find that land is still ahead of it? If a child boasts that he has as many clothes as his father, can he equally boast of having as many rags as his father?

'And you, Titus, you must listen to the words of my mouth. Where Simeon tells you to go, you must go. Where he tells you there is no way, know there is no way; turn back. Associate with the men he tells you are safe. Avoid those he points out to you as dangerous. Let the eyes of Simeon be your eyes from this day on; let his hands be your hands. Does the thread not follow the path made by the needle?

'It is in spite of the snake that the bush rat nurtures its young to maturity. Regardless of the activities of

6

human snakes, you Simeon will pilot your child Titus to success in Government work . . .'

'Amen, Amen,' the crowd chorused.

'Simeon and Titus, anyone that pries too much into the secrets between you two will have his eyes scorched by fire. May he go blind.'

'Amen, Amen.'

'Whoever comes between the two of you will be ground to pulp in a motor accident.'

'Amen, Amen.'

'Amen. It must be so. For I speak these words at dawn. And, and – where is the dish I asked you to get ready, Deborah?' Joel said in a serious aside to Deborah. One of the women entered one of the four rooms opening out into the parlour. She brought out an enamel dish which she held before the old man kneeling. Old Joel selected a big kola nut from inside it.

'This is a kola nut,' he announced to the group who were perfectly aware what it was. 'With this kola nut I invoke the spirit of Oluode to come to our midst. I know that you, Oluode, our great ancestor, are now with us. I can see you, because I am an old man and I shall soon qualify to come to you; these others cannot see you because they are still young. Those of them that are not young are women, that is why they cannot see you. I call you to be witness of the vow that these two descendants of yours make at this solemn hour, before cockcrow.'

He split the nut into four. He bit off a piece from one of the quarters and chewed it solemnly. They all watched its disappearance into his stomach as the lump went down his throat. He broke what was left of this same quarter into two and handed a piece each to Simeon and Titus and ordered them each to eat.

'Treachery is a deadly sin. Oluode our ancestor who

7

is now with us does not tolerate it,' he warned gravely. 'A brother that shares kola with a brother and engages in an act that can lead his brother to trouble commits treachery. He incurs the displeasure of Oluode. Oluode never forgives treachery.'

Titus had begun to have a strange feeling, curiously enough, from the moment that the old man had said that Oluode was present with them and was watching the proceedings. The scene with so many women and a few men gathered under the dim light in that ghostly hour of the day was eerie enough. Titus began to have the feeling that he was gradually coming under some strange influence that he could not explain. Something deep down in him was telling him in a thin voice that he should break away from it all – he felt that he should run out of the airless room into the fresh atmosphere outside – an atmosphere that was free of ancestral spirits. But he found himself completely powerless to carry out his desire. He saw himself unable to resist whatever he was ordered to do by his old great-uncle. He watched the old man, as in a dream pour out some water from a gourd into a calabash.

'This is water from the stream that flows past our ancestral village,' the old man said, drinking out of the calabash. 'It is water from the tears of the eyes of Oluode our ancestor,' he added, offering the calabash to Simeon. 'I brought it down myself, for this very purpose.'

Titus noticed that Simeon handed the calabash back to old Joel. He noticed old Joel hand it to him, saying something which was inaudible and incomprehensible to him. He saw himself drinking – drinking, drinking. Then for a long time afterwards, Titus Oti, Bachelor of Science (Engineering), graduate of the University of London, remembered nothing.

Two

---◇---

Two days after his strange dawn-of-morning introduction to his kinsman Simeon, Titus Oti was back at Ibadan, the regional capital, for an interview with the Regional Director of the Government Department of Public Works. He was shown in by an elderly messenger in khaki.

'Ah, Mr O'Tay. Welcome back to your own country. I hope you had a pleasant voyage.'

'Quite pleasant, thank you, sir,' Titus said shouting the last word as he leapt to one side in fright, avoiding a white spaniel that had yelped at him in unmistakable unfriendliness, and had made for the leg of his trousers.

'Come, come, Caesar. Still. No, quite still, Caesar,' the old man said in affectionate rebuke to the dog. 'Time you knew friend from foe, Caesar. Sit down, there. That's better. I must apologize for the grossly bad manners of Caesar, O'Tay,' he said offering his hand. 'When he gets to know you, you will find that he's the sweetest representative of the canine tribe. But tell me, O'Tay, how did you come by an Irish name?'

'My name is not Irish, sir,' Titus explained. 'It is Oti, not O'Tay. And it is Yoruba.'

'Not Irish, I see. My mistake, I'm sure. Where were you at College, O'Tay?'

'King's College, sir, London University.'

'Queen's College? I thought that's in Ireland, O'Tay?'

'King's College, sir. Not Queen's.'

'King's, I see. My hearing is a little defective, O'Tay. So bear with me if I don't hear you first time. I'm not exactly a young man as you can see,' and he laughed enthusiastically as if his misfortune of defective hearing was an additional professional qualification to which the young recruit to his empire could aspire to attain only after many years of engineering practice. 'Quite a few boys from King's have joined us lately. Another score against their traditional rivals of the Godless institution at Gower Street, eh?'

The joke escaped Titus. He did not like dogs. He certainly did not like this particular one called Caesar. He kept an eye on him all the time. He saw that Caesar also kept an eye on him. There was no doubting that the dislike and mistrust was mutual.

'You were at King's for how many years, O'Tay?'

'Three years, sir.'

'Splendid, Splendid. A good pass degree, I imagine? Good, quite good.' He beamed with enthusiasm. Titus noticed that he was well past middle age. He was thick-set, with a double chin. He was quite hairy, his skin having acquired the brownish tan usual with Englishmen that have lived many years in a tropical climate.

'And you've been training under an engineer on the Index of the Institution of Civil Engineers, O'Tay?'

'Quite so, sir. County Surveyor of Essex.'

'Under whom?'

'The County Surveyor, Essex County Council, sir.'

'Joe Powell,' he cried. 'We were together in the

Marines in the 1914–18 War. Of course he's in Sussex. Of course he is.'

Titus left the embarrassing mistake just as he had ignored the mistake about his name. While the Director attended to a telephone call he looked round the room. There was a map of Nigeria on the wall, with thick red lines indicating the trunk roads, the responsibility of the Public Works Department. Tiny aeroplane symbols in red indicated the airports, another responsibility of the Department. There was a chart next to the map. He discovered that it was a posting chart, with the names and places to which the men were posted. All the names were non-Nigerian: Johnson, Beattie, McBain, Graham-Jones, Owen, and so on, not one Nigerian. For he, Titus Oti, was the first professionally qualified Nigerian civil engineer to join the Service. He noticed that there were a number of blanks against certain place names. These were the vacancies. He had been told by the Director of Colonial Scholars in London that the Department was desperately short of engineers and that the Nigerian Government was very anxious that he should get back home quickly to fill one of the vacancies.

'Did you have a good design experience, O'Tay?' the Director asked, scribbling something on a file before him.

'Yes, sir,' Titus said after some hesitation, which escaped the old man.

'Designed any bridges? I imagine you wouldn't have much chance of designing new bridges down in Sussex. I was reading in the Institution's journal the other day that Parliament was considering proposals for reconstructing the London–Birmingham trunk road. That would be a wonderful opportunity for younger engineers to have design experience. You can design culverts, can't you?'

'Yes, sir.'

'That will be all you will need to know. All our bridges here have been designed by the Crown Agents. You have to be familiar with the Crown Agents' standard spans and their specifications.' He wrote a few more notes in the file before him.

'And when you were in England, O'Tay,' the Director said, looking at Titus penetratingly, 'did you move about much? Were you able to see something of our British way of life? Were you able to stay with English men and women in their own homes, O'Tay?'

'That I certainly did, sir, thanks to the British Council.'

'And you no doubt discovered that the Englishman is a human being, possessed of flesh and blood like you, and not the ogre that your nationalist papers here paint him to be? Englishmen were kind to you, were they not?'

'Yes, they were, sir,' Titus answered looking at the old man. He knew then that he was telling only part, and not the whole truth. Some Englishmen were good, very good to him. A good number were quite bad, very bad. But the vast majority were completely unmindful of his existence and showed not the slightest interest in him and his affairs. But just now at his first meeting with his Director he was not going into the vexed subject of the colour-bar in Britain.

The Director knocked the ashes out of his pipe and changed the pipe for another from a battery of four on his desk. He proceeded to charge the new pipe with tobacco from a tin on the desk. He lit the pipe and sucked it tenderly for a moment. Then he called someone on the intercom.

'Where's O'Tay the new arrival from Britain posted? Ibadan – Oyo Province?' he said appearing surprised. 'I thought we decided the next arrival was to go to Abeokuta. The telegram, of course I quite forgot . . .

going to McBain, then . . . Right . . . Quite . . . quite.'

Replacing the receiver he said, 'Dick McBain is Scottish to the core, O'Tay, he's your Provincial Engineer. You will find him a good specimen of his tribe. It requires a Scotsman to put the finances of the Province in order. My dear O'Tay, the first and last thing in your career in the P.W.D. is the control of expenditure. Over-expenditure is criminal in engineering.' He puffed at his pipe, contemplating Titus. He stretched out his hand to him. 'O'Tay, if ever you want my advice do not hesitate to come to me. Good morning, and good luck.'

As Titus rose to go out, Caesar growled.

Three

---◇---

TITUS stayed in Ibadan till evening attending to this and to that. He was struck by the extreme sluggishness of the clerks at headquarters and the very slow pace at which they attended to the various papers concerning him which went from officer to officer. He was required to sign his appointment papers. Headquarters knew he had arrived two days before. They had themselves written to him a letter which he had received on the boat in Freetown instructing him to call to see the Director that very morning and to call at the office of the Assistant Chief Clerk in charge of personnel to sign his appointment papers after seeing the Director.

'Yes?' A sullen-looking clerk looked up from a file in front of him. 'This is the office of the A.C.C. Personnel. Do you want to see him?'

'Yes, I do. He is expecting me,' Titus said, irritated.

'What is your name that I can tell him when he comes back?'

'Is he not in then?' Titus asked, disappointed.

'He is on sick leave.'

'Sick leave! Well, isn't there someone else who does his duties when he's away?'

'I'm acting for him here.'

'Then you should know about the appointment he arranged for me for this morning. My name is Oti, Titus Oti.'

'Oh, I'm pleased to know you, Mr Oti. But what is the nature of your business?'

'The nature of my business?' Titus asked in unconcealed anger. 'Did you yourself in this office not write this letter saying that I should come to this office to sign my appointment papers this morning?' He stuck the letter before the nose of the vice-A.C.C.

'Oh! You are the new engineer that has just come back from U.K.! Welcome, sir. Welcome, sir,' he greeted him enthusiastically after realizing his importance. 'I shall call for your file, sir. Please sit down, sir. Please sit down, sir. I shall go for it myself from the filing depot.'

After eventually getting through the signing of his appointment papers he decided to go and cable his safe arrival to Bola, his fiancée, in London. Most students travelling back from the United Kingdom to Nigeria arrive safely in Nigeria without incident. But it was the custom that the day after you arrived you cabled back to say the obvious in the most expensive way.

He stood on the concrete steps of the pavement of the grey headquarters building, perplexed. The official Vanguard Estate car that had been assigned to him did not appear to be around. Nor the driver. He saw several other cars parked in front of the building. But where was his?

'You want your car, sir?' A messenger approached him.

'Yes, I do,' he confirmed.

'Layi, Layi,' he shouted. 'Engineer want you. You go play with woman under mango tree you lef your work. Na today dem de sack you.'

The driver emerged in confusion from under the

mango tree. He ran to Titus. He explained in Yoruba that he had parked the car round the corner under the shade of a tree that it might be cool and comfortable 'for master'.

He sat immediately behind the driver, and told him to drive to the Post Office. As he was manoeuvring the car out of the headquarters grounds the driver advised him that he should move to the 'owner's' corner in the back seat of the car. Only small people who were not important sat with the driver in front or immediately behind him in a car. He was an engineer – a very important man.

After spending some irritating twelve minutes in one of several very slow-moving queues at the General Post Office he eventually reached the head of the queue. He asked the clerk behind the counter for a cable form. Without looking up from some entry which he was completing in respect of his last customer the clerk said, irritated: 'Cable! Why don't you go to the Cable Office instead of wasting my time? Next please.'

'I beg your pardon?' Titus asked, truly perplexed.

'Go to the Cable Office,' a female voice shouted from behind him.

'You are wasting our time,' another man said, also from behind him.

'Push him aside, *o jare*,' the woman again said in Yoruba. 'Judging from the way he wears a suit and tie in this hot weather you would think that he would know a Post Office from a Cable Office.'

Titus fixed her with an unfriendly stare. 'Just what have I done to you, woman, that you should talk about me in this abusive way?' he asked her in Yoruba.

'*Ye. Jesu!*' she exclaimed. 'So you do understand Yoruba?' she asked coyly. They all laughed at the embarrassing situation. 'The way you refused to answer my greetings when I said "*E karo o*" and the way you tightened your face and looked in the air made me conclude you are a *kobokobo*. Don't be cross with me, my dear.' She was enchanting, he thought.

'I see you have just come back from England?' the counter-clerk said, looking at his brown suit more critically. 'We do not do cables here in the Post Office. You go to Cable and Wireless. Farther up Lagos Road.'

'At the junction of Cable Street and Lagos Road,' the woman said, now showing definite interest in the Johnny-just-come.

'And what can I do for you, Auntie?' the clerk asked of the woman who had jumped the queue. Titus murmured a 'thank you' to her as he was going out of the Post Office. He told the driver to drive to the Cable Office.

He transacted his business at the Cable Office without any hitch. As he was being handed the five shillings receipt slip by the counter-clerk, Simeon his kinsman came in.

'Remember I told you I would come to Ibadan with you today, D.E.?' the man said to the hearing of all and to the embarrassment of Titus. 'When I sent round to the house I was informed that you had left. Then I immediately set out in my car. Unfortunately I had engine trouble on the way. Seven miles from Ibala.'

'Oh, yes? Is the car all right now?' Titus asked, leading the way out of the Cable Office.

'Oh, yes. It is quite all right now, D.E. By the way, did you have quick attention here? I know the General Manager. I shall introduce you. He is a member of the All Races Club. We must go there now, for lunch. The food is quite good.'

Titus had made no arrangements for lunch so he gladly accepted his cousin's suggestion.

Simeon handed his keys to the driver of the official car and instructed him to drive his own old Austin A40 to the Club. He himself slid into the driver's seat of the Vanguard. Titus sat at his side. He noticed that Simeon drove rather badly as they went up Lagos Road. He thought he probably was not familiar with the controls of the Vanguard.

On the way Simeon explained that he had been to headquarters looking for him and that he had been told by the clerks there that Titus had finished his business there and that none of them knew where he had gone. It was a messenger on the ground floor that had heard the new engineer instruct his driver to go to the General Post Office. At the Post Office he had been told that Titus had been and gone, and that he should try the Cable Office.

Titus told him of his disappointment at the very poor service both at headquarters and at the Post Office. Simeon explained that it was just for that reason that he had decided to come with him to Ibadan.

'They don't know you yet; that's the trouble. When they know you and what you are, you will see that you will get anything you want anywhere. I had meant to introduce you to the people at headquarters myself. The Chief Clerk and the Administrative Assistant are both members of the Club. At the Post Office the Deputy Postmaster is also a member of the Club. He's a European, you know. But he's unlike the other Europeans. He likes Africans. As a matter of fact he has an African wife.'

'Oh yes.'

'You must meet him. I shall introduce you to him,' he said, as he cut the corner in a most dangerous way driving into the All Races Club. He parked equally badly near a big Chevrolet. 'Good, very good. Mr

Suleiman is here,' Simeon said as he and Titus climbed out of the car. 'This is his Chev. One of the most powerful people in Ibadan. He also owns half the houses in Isale Eko in Lagos. He is a big transporter. . . . That Opel Kapitan belongs to Chief Owolabi. The car at the end there belongs to Barrister Williams. He won it off Chief Owolabi here at the Club.'

'People gamble extensively here, then?' Titus asked. He did not hear Simeon's reply which was drowned in shouts of 'Uncle, Uncle', as Simeon led his visitor to a crowd of people seated round a bar. Simeon introduced him to them one by one: 'This is my cousin, Mr Titus Oti, B.Sc. (Eng.). He's the new District Engineer of Ibala.'

Titus shook hands round. Black hands, white hands; male hands, female hands. There were several offers of drinks: Gin and bitters? Whisky and soda? Beer – which brand?

'Squash – rubbish, woman's stuff,' one of the men said. Titus did not remember his name. 'Be a man. Take a man's drink. Make it a beer at least. Steward, Heineken's for Mr Oti.'

'No thank you', he said calmly. 'Orange squash if I may.'

'And you, Uncle?' the transporter asked. 'A double whisky and soda?'

Simeon nodded assent.

The drinks were brought to them when they had sat down at a table in the little dining-room. Titus found it an infinite relief to be here and not at the bar where tobacco smoke hung heavily in the air. He noticed that a couple sat on one of the tables. The girl appeared to be shy. The man had hailed their entrance by shouting 'Uncle'.

Simeon went out for a few minutes. In that time Titus

thought of many things. Of the Director of Public Works. Of the slow service at the headquarters and at the Post Office. Of the woman at the Post Office. Of his cousin Simeon and of the circle to which he had introduced him. Then Simeon entered followed by the transporter.

'Mr Suleiman, this is my cousin Mr Titus Oti, B.Sc. (Eng.). I have introduced him once to you but I think you need more than one introduction. And D. E., this is Mr Suleiman. He is the biggest transporter in Ibadan and Lagos. He is a most friendly person.'

Titus spilt the remains of his drink in the confusion of this unexpected second introduction. 'Steward, another squash for this woman engineer,' Mr Suleiman said. 'Only women drink squash. Women, and bad men!'

'Mr Suleiman, as I told you, is a member of the Committee. He has consented to be your Chief Proposer. You see he has already signed the application form,' Simeon said showing Titus an illegible signature on a form headed 'All Races Club'. 'I shall get the General Manager of U.A.C. to be the second proposer.'

'No,' Suleiman said. 'Not him. It must be my friend the Regional Manager of the Nigerian Railway. You sign here, and I shall take it to him this evening.'

During the meal Simeon explained to his cousin the wonderful advantages of associating with people that matter and the enormous benefits of membership of the All Races Club. Titus listened to it all and wondered.

Four

---◇---

RICHARD McBAIN, Provincial Engineer of the Department of Public Works, Ibadan, had been most disappointed at the official letter from headquarters informing him that a new arrival, a Nigerian by the name of Oti, had been posted to his Province to take over Ibala District. And when Titus reported at his office, three days after the interview with the Director at headquarters, McBain did not conceal his disappointment from the new arrival. Titus thought that even the pleasantries that one normally exchanges with a new colleague, whom one is meeting for the first time, did not come readily to him.

'So headquarters has sent you to take over Ibala District, Mr Oti?' he asked, without expecting an answer and not leaving enough time for one before going on. 'I had asked for someone experienced in both labour control and in financial control. I see this is your first tour, Mr Oti?'

Titus nodded. He did not speak. Something told him he should not speak much to this unfriendly person.

'I am afraid you will not find things here as easy as your college professors made you believe they were, back home in the University. You will find them not exactly answering to the methods you learnt in Differential Calculus and Theory of Structures and Fluid Mechanics – all the stuff in the books. Here you will be dealing with men, money and materials. And here in Nigeria you will find that all three behave most strangely.'

He exploded in a sneeze. The telephone rang. 'Dick McBain here. . . . Yes, Alan . . . Yes, yes, next Sunday . . . . Sure, that will be fine. . . . Hope you are proposing an amendment to Rule 25 at the Annual Meeting on Saturday? Time we checked the irresponsibility of chaps who convert the Club into a children's playground. Disgraceful what's happening . . .'

Titus regarded his new boss with misgiving; he knew he was not going to like him. He had entertained no illusion as to the career he'd chosen being without difficulties and frustrations. But need this man rub it in?

'You smoke, Mr Oti?' And before Titus had had time to reply he had made up his mind for him. 'More sensible than most, I see. Good, good.' He lit himself a cigarette after he had tapped its end three times on the match-box.

Titus spoke. 'Just one thing, Mr McBain. I rather gather that I'm being posted to be District Engineer, Ibala.'

'Yes, Mr Oti?'

'That means I'll have to live in Ibala?'

'Well, don't you want to?'

'No, I don't. I wonder if I can be posted to some other duty that will not make it necessary to live in Ibala.'

'No. I'm afraid that's absolutely impossible. You see I asked for someone to be District Engineer, Ibala. And headquarters has sent you here to be District Engineer, Ibala. Frankly speaking, I don't care a hoot who goes to Ibala so long as he's honest and can keep his accounts straight. You should have sorted all this out at headquarters.' He regarded Titus for a moment before he asked: 'And why, may I ask, don't you want to live in Ibala?'

'Ibala is my home-town.'

'Ah, then accept my congratulations on your good fortune, Mr Oti. I was not so lucky in my first or subsequent tours. The nearest posting to my home-town has been four thousand miles.'

Titus did not appreciate the humour. The telephone rang again. 'McBain, P.W.D. Yes, what? Listen, cock; this is P.W.D. not P. & T.' And with that he banged the receiver. He looked at Titus in a vacant sort of way. Apparently he was trying to remember the point at which the conversation had been interrupted.

'I was saying that I don't want to live in Ibala.'

'Your home-town.'

'Yes, my home-town. This is a matter about which I feel very strongly. My people would make my work nearly impossible. They would descend upon me in large numbers at all hours of the day. They'd want this – they'd want that. It's something that an Englishman cannot understand, Mr McBain.'

'Scotsman, my friend,' he corrected haughtily. 'You and I are one in our objective, Mr Oti: the total destruction of the imperialist dragon.' He continued after a pause: 'In that direction I must admit that you are here succeeding better than we in Scotland, even though we have been fighting the common enemy much longer than you.'

'Can't you change the posting?' Titus was insistent.

'Impossible. Absolutely impossible. Unless, of course, you wish to forward a petition to headquarters – through me – on the subject. I shall put it to headquarters – with my comments. . . . Meanwhile, the Chief Clerk will issue to you – and you will sign for – one number

23

Financial Instructions, one number *Government of Nigeria General Orders*. These are the two testaments of the Civil Service Bible, Mr Oti. They are to be read together with circulars and other instructions that come from headquarters and from this office from time to time – Mr GEO - RR - GE!', he shouted in a way that made Titus nearly jump to his feet.

'Yes, sir!' someone shouted in reply from the next-door room. The man came in. He was grey-haired. He wore glasses, and a shirt without a collar. His figure was reminiscent of Dickens' Mr Pickwick. And, like Pickwick, he suspended his pantaloons from his shoulders with a pair of braces that were the worse for wear.

'Yes, sir?' the man repeated in obvious awe of the Provincial Engineer.

'One copy *Financial Instructions*, one copy *General Orders* for Mr Oti, District Engineer, Ibala. See that the book is duly signed.'

'Yes, sir.'

'That is all, Mr George.'

'Yes, sir,' the Chief Clerk said and disappeared.

'The District Engineer's house at Ibala was redecorated just before you arrived. You will find it is in excellent condition. I'm still trying to sort out the claim sent in by the contractor for the redecoration. It was certified correct by the Foreman. You will have to keep an eye on that Foreman, Mr Oti. . . . And oh, Mr Oti, about this invitation here, kind of your family to have invited me to the thanksgiving service next Sunday. But I'm already booked to play golf with the Resident. My apologies to all concerned. Ian McLapperton, the Yard Superintendent, will be there. He will represent both the P.W.D. and the Highland Scots.'

Five

---◇---

THE morning service at All Souls Church, Ibala, the following Sunday, was a special one for the family of Sister Deborah. A combined memorial service for her late husband and a thanksgiving service for the safe return of her son Titus from England. Sister Deborah and her relatives and friends filled the first five pews reserved for them in the middle block, and overflowed into the next few pews both in the middle block and the side blocks.

The Rev. Michael Morakinyo read out the first of his two texts from the Book of Revelation, Chapter 14, verse 13: 'I heard a voice from heaven, saying unto me, Write. From henceforth blessed are the dead which die in the Lord . . . for they rest from their labours.' He read it a second time after surveying his congregation and nodding inward satisfaction. The church was filled to capacity. Not just quantity in attendance; there was quality as well. For a number of important sons of the soil had come home to Ibala from Lagos and Ibadan for this great occasion in which the town and the church formally welcomed back the first Ibala man to be a qualified engineer. It meant that the special thanksgiving collection and the normal church collection during the singing of the last hymn would be substantial.

He cleared his throat as he launched forth upon a biography of the late Samuel Oti. He emphasized how he was a veritable pillar of All Souls Church. He was the President of the Society of the Good Samaritans for nine years in all of which time he gave an excellent example of leadership and hospitality, worthy of a true follower of the good Samaritan of the Bible. He was for the last three years of his life the church's lay delegate to the Diocesan Synod in Lagos and he was a worthy representative too. His financial support for the work of God was always an inspiration to all who came in contact with him.

'The promise of blessedness is not for all that die,' the preacher announced to his congregation, fixing his eyes on the organist. 'It is only the dead which die in the Lord that are blessed,' he explained. 'It is only those that die in the fear of the Lord after having lived the life of a good Christian here on earth! Our records here in this church testify to the fact that our dearly beloved Elder Samuel Oti lived in the fear of the Lord. He died, in harness, a good and true Christian soldier in the army of his royal Master and Saviour. Henceforth is laid up for him a crown of glory, at the side of his Saviour, where in the company of others that had gone to glory before him he now sings: Glory, glory, glory, Lord God of Hosts!'

To Sister Deborah and the rest of the bereaved family the preacher addressed special words of comfort and consolation, which evoked sobs from a number of places in the front five pews and from elsewhere in the church. He urged his dear Sister Deborah to believe in the Lord and in the Resurrection.

'Christians,' he quoted, 'live for ever and love for ever, but they never part for ever.' If Sister Deborah believed in the Lord of the Resurrection she was sure to meet her husband on the Resurrection Day. Elder Samuel was parted from her and from the rest of the family and from the church of All Souls only for a little while. Her greatest comfort should be in this knowledge of the great Day of Reunion. Elder Samuel Oti, President of the Society of Good Samaritans, had only gone ahead to prepare places for Sister Deborah, for Engineer Titus, and for members of his society.

He mopped his brow, looked round the congregation and continued, 'Man proposes but God disposes. When five years ago he bade his son young Titus good-bye he little knew that it was to be good-bye for ever.' This was greeted with renewed sobbing. He continued,

'We are all sorry that he has not lived to this day to see his son return from England, a great man starting on a great career in the service of his country and of his God. We who are left behind this side of Jordan wonder why it has pleased God to call unto him Elder Samuel before the return of Engineer Titus. But the Lord our God who knows all things past, present and future, the Lord God that knows best when to harvest His wheat and when to call in His own, decided that the home call of the father must precede the home-coming of the son. And I ask you: who are we mortals to seek to know the whys and wherefores of the doings of the Lord our God, *Oba a sere ma se ka?*'

He again mopped his brow before continuing. 'When a fire goes out its face is covered with ashes,' he quoted the first half of a popular Yoruba proverb. 'When the banana plant dies it is succeeded by its suckers. When we die may we have worthy children to replace us.'

A great 'amen' was chorused from all corners of the church. One elderly woman went somewhat farther than the rest and shouted to the embarrassment and amusement of those in her immediate neighbourhood, 'Lord Jesus

27

please let me be succeeded by my children when I die, that I may not die in disgrace – I come to church every Sunday.'

The preacher continued, 'We rejoice today in the knowledge that Elder Samuel has died leaving behind a suitable replacement and worthy son in the person of Engineer Titus. It is our prayer as a church that he may live long to be a worthy successor and replacement for his great father both in the church and in the family.'

He congratulated Titus Oti on his brilliant achievement of being the first Ibala son and one of the very first Nigerians to qualify as an engineer. He confessed that he did not know the details of the studies one went through before qualifying to be an engineer. He knew that one of the subjects one had to study was called mathematics. It was a terribly difficult subject. So difficult that it affected the brains of students. A number of Nigerians who had embarked upon engineering studies had been mentally afflicted and had become serious problems to their families and to Government. So anyone who completed his engineering studies and still kept his brain intact must be specially congratulated.

He made another confession. He had not been to the white man's country. But he had heard and read stories about the many dangers that beset the African student. Cold, terrible cold. Shortage of food, at least of the kind to which the student was accustomed at home. His congregation cried in astonishment when he gave out the confidential information that Titus Oti had not eaten a single meal of pounded yam with okro soup for all the five years he was away in Britain till the night he returned home! Then there were pretty girls – white girls who lured away the unwary student from his studies. 'A student that battles successfully against all these dangers and comes back home with glory deserves to be praised.

He has not shamed his race.' He stopped for a breath. He looked round his congregation. It had swollen further since he started the sermon in spite of the standing regulation against admitting anyone into the church after the sermon had started. Ecclesiastical disapproval momentarily flickered on his face at the ostentatiousness of a number of women in the middle of the second row. The bright clothes and sparkling trinkets contrasted sharply with the simple attire of a woman church member who at that time was hard put to it trying to smother the wailing of her infant.

The preacher read out his second text from the ninth chapter of the Book of Proverbs, verse 10: 'The fear of the Lord is the beginning of wisdom, and the knowledge of the Holy One is understanding.' He read it a second time. He said that all education, all knowledge without the fear of the Lord amounted to nothing. There were some people who after acquiring much knowledge said that they no longer believed in the existence of God. 'But mere belief in the existence of God is not enough. The true Christian must be both a believer and a doer, living the way the Lord his Saviour had decreed, living a clean life full of worship, full of charity, supporting at all times the work of God.

'Engineer Titus has not had time to look round, but even from where he is sitting now he can see through the window the gigantic structure going up, evidence that while he has been away passing his examinations and winning glory for us his church and his race, we stay-at-homes have not been sleeping. We have laid the foundations of a new temple to the glory of God, a temple worthy of the name of the great Jehovah and of all the saints. We are all confident that Titus Oti, son of Elder Samuel Oti the good, who was a tower of strength in this church, will give most generously to the building fund of the church where he was once a choir-boy. . . .'

After the singing of the post-sermon hymn the pastor announced that the wives and children, the relatives and well-wishers of the late Elder Samuel Oti should come forward in a body to the altar for blessing. They all trooped out, led by the old man Joel, and followed by Sister Deborah, Titus and all the rest. With the exception of old Joel, who was forbidden by custom to show any ostentation on such an occasion, they were all most gorgeously dressed. Sister Deborah's outfit of *Sanyan iro* over an off-white serge *buba*, with yards of *sanyan gele* on her head and stylish Italian sandals on her feet, easily cut off a good ten years from her age. Her gold necklace, bangles and ear-rings looked expensive. She herself looked radiant.

Simeon Oke of the P.W.D. was most conspicuous in his double role of relative of the dead and church leader. He wore an expensive *sanyan* robe with voluminous folds and long gold chain round his neck. As unofficial master of ceremonies it was he who beckoned to this relative to stand here and that well-wisher to stay there, at the altar rail. It was he who piloted the sole European worshipper to the altar and showed him where to kneel down next to Titus. That worthy sweated profusely in his blue-black wool suit. To the singing of the first two verses of a popular Easter hymn the pastor and Simeon Oke passed round the collection plates among the kneeling crowd.

The crowd had hardly resumed their seats when the pastor made another announcement. The family and friends and well-wishers of Engineer Titus Oti, B.Sc. (Eng.) (London) would now come forward to the altar for thanksgiving and blessing. Up went the same crowd again, trooping out once more to the altar, and everyone, pastor, wardens, worshippers, going through the same processes all over again. Everyone except the sole European worshipper, Ian McLapperton, who sweated in embarrassment and confusion. He had not known that offertory was to be made more than once and had dropped a 10s note in the plate on the earlier occasion, to the delight of the pastor and admiration of all who saw him do it. He now ransacked his clothes for his wallet – the breast pocket, the jacket right pocket, the left – no luck. Then back to the breast pocket, the two jacket pockets – still no luck. Trousers right pocket, trousers left – still no luck. Trousers seat pocket – ah, he located it! He hurriedly dragged out a red note, a £1 note, which he quickly placed apologetically in the plate the pastor had held patiently before him.

It was at that moment that Titus saw her, and his heart missed a beat. She wore a cream woollen *buba* round the lower end of which she wrapped a well-laundered *iro* of the same material. Her *gele* appeared from the distance to be silk, about two yards of it, and of the same colour as her *buba* and *iro*. Her shoes were brown with high heels. Her trinkets were not too conspicuous; they were adequate and elegant. Recollection came to Titus. The woman the post-office clerk had called Auntie, who had addressed him rudely at the Post Office in Ibadan. Now in Ibala. Was she a relative? Was she a well-wisher of the family?

Six

———————◇———————

TITUS was cross with his mother and he told her so. 'How many times will I tell you that if you want to come and see me you should send someone to tell me. I'll come to fetch you in my car. Do you have to walk from one end of the town to the other to get to me here at the Government Reservation? And now you are soaking wet.'

His mother in her turn was cross with him. 'Whenever I come to you you scold me as if I'm a little child of yesterday. I'm not. If it was not important for me to come I would not have come. And do I complain to you that I'm tired of walking? It's my feet and not yours that I use – why do you have to complain?' She paused to concentrate on the important business of unstrapping an infant from her back. It clung for security to the part of her *buba* round her bosom. She succeeded in depositing it on the floor. It took immediate possession of its new kingdom and crawled all over the place. It had no clothes on whatsoever.

Titus followed the baby round with a disapproving eye. 'Whose child is it, Mother?'

'The child of Rachel, the daughter of your father's elder sister. You remember her; she was at the thanksgiving service.' Deborah was in the habit of measuring dates and describing people from the time of the thanksgiving service and the attendance at the thanksgiving service.

'But look at that, Mother. See what a mess the baby has made on the floor,' Titus cried in anger. The baby had first urinated on the carpet and then had proceeded to play with the mess.

'But, Titus, why must you be angry that a baby has done this? Does it know any better – does it know that it is wrong?'

'I don't care what it knows and what it does not know. I want you to take it away from here, now.'

'Did you not do worse when you were a child?'

He opened his mouth and without saying a thing snapped it shut in anger.

She smiled in triumph, and proceeded to press home her obvious advantage. 'Is it not the prayer of everybody that he may have the good fortune of having a child that will both urinate and evacuate its bowels on his clothes and on his mat? And when you have settled down sufficiently and Bola has come back from the white man's country too and you are both married, will you not pray to have a child like this that will urinate and vomit all over the house?'

'No,' he said in monosyllabic finality.

'My God, Titus,' she cried in anguish. 'You must not curse yourself. You will have a child. You will have not just one but several children. And I am going to tend them all on this back of mine.'

'Yes, I pray I'll have children, but not the sort we are talking about now. Not one without a napkin on. And tell me now what the important matter is that has brought you here.'

'This letter,' she said. She untied the knot at one corner

of her head-tie. She brought out a crumpled envelope which she handed to him. He frowned; he noticed that half the address on the envelope had been rendered illegible by water. He tore it open and brought out the sheet of paper inside.

'Pastor and Foreman told me it is very important,' she said as he began to read the note. 'So I decided to bring it myself.'

Very important, sure enough. Addressed to Titus Oti, Esq., B.Sc. (Eng.) (London), it was from the Harvest Committee of All Souls Church. It said that the Committee had unanimously elected him to be the Chief Opener at the Bazaar Sale that year. They were writing him formally to acquaint him with this decision. The Committee would be calling on him at his convenience to discuss details. The note ended with a reminder of the good things that the Lord of the Harvest had in store for those who contributed generously to both the Harvest and the Bazaar.

She noticed the frown on his face. 'What has Pastor written in the letter, Titus?'

'He and his Harvest Committee want me to open the Bazaar Sales.'

'They want you to open the Bazaar Sales!' she echoed. 'That is going to be serious. I don't want you to be exposed to the glare of the public yet, Titus.'

Titus shared her anxiety. For once mother and son appeared to agree.

'When women who are older than I see you performing this very important function they will be jealous, because their own sons are not as important as my son. That is why I am anxious. I am afraid of witches and evil-doers.'

Titus listened to her, but said nothing.

'But we must accept the invitation since it has something to do with the church' – she appeared to be having second thoughts. 'If we don't, they will think we are running away from spending money. We must begin to prepare for it now.'

'What do we prepare – and how many of us?' he asked, staring at the baby who at that time was laying waste everything movable in its path.

'Well, must we not begin to prepare for it now? Is it not going to cost money, much money?'

'About how much?'

'Can you do it for less than £30? When your kinsman, the Foreman, did it last year he opened it with more than that. He spent about £40.'

'More than £30! Where did he get the money from?' he asked without really expecting her to give the answer.

'He is quite rich, Titus. And you too will soon be rich. You both do the same work and people who do this work have plenty of money. Everyone says so. And I know it's true.'

'But, Mother, I don't want you to talk like this,' he stopped her. 'I have no money, and I'm going to be honest. I'm not going to steal any money, to please anyone. If the Church people want £30 from me for opening Bazaar Sales, they will be disappointed. I just haven't got it.'

'But, Titus, you mustn't talk like that. You mustn't let down the family. We shall find the money.'

'And please pick up the child, Mother. It's messed up the floor enough. Thomas has brought some food for you. Drink the Ovaltine. It will do you good. After that I'll drive you back home. How's my great-aunt today?'

'She is well. But people of her age die without warning – without being ill. So you must begin to put money aside now for the funeral expenses.'

'Money for Bazaar Sales! Money for funeral expenses!

Money for this, money for that. Christ in heaven! It's nothing but money, money, and yet more money ever since I came back from England!'

'Titus!'

On the drive back to his mother's home Titus pondered the problem of money and allied matters. Before he left England he had been told at the Colonial Office that his salary on arrival in Nigeria would be forty-two pounds ten shillings a month. He and Bola had thought that that was a reasonably good salary and that he should be able to save at least twelve pounds ten shillings out of this every month. Surely one pound a day was sufficient to live on.

He had been back from England five months now. And in every one of these five months there had been demands on his purse. One pound a day had not been sufficient to live on at all. What really made the cost of living higher than he expected was the extra expenses of a cook-steward, Thomas. He paid him four pounds a month; but he made nearly as much again on the purchases he made at the market and in pilfering. He resented intensely Deborah's attempts to take over the buying of foodstuffs for her son. In this he was well supported by his master! Finally, Titus himself ate only a mere fraction of the food Thomas cooked. Thomas saw to it that more than enough was cooked – the rest being eaten by him and his tribal brothers.

'Look out, look out,' his mother shouted in panic. He saw it, nearly too late, he swerved sharply to the left bringing the car to a screeching stop mere inches short of a telegraph pole on the off-side of the road. He had very narrowly avoided a head-on collision with a lorry. He had mistaken the oncoming vehicle for a motor-cycle because it had only a single headlamp, which the driver had not dipped. It was at the last minute that the 'motor-cycle' had suddenly materialized into a lorry – with near-disastrous consequences.

'*Jesu! Jesu!*' Deborah cried in fright.

Titus climbed out of his car, fuming. The driver of the lorry had stopped. He too came out, and shouted: 'Why won't you drive carefully? You nearly ran into my lorry.'

'You must be mad, you senseless idiot,' Titus answered him, shaking with rage and from the shock of the averted accident.

'Don't you call me an idiot, I tell you,' the driver cried. 'And don't you tell me I'm mad. There is no madness in my family history. You appear to be a big man. This is the only reason why I refrain from calling you mad yourself.'

'Why on earth don't you have both headlights working properly?'

'The other one is not working. The mechanic tried to get it working but it just wouldn't work. And what am I to do, Mother?' he appealed to Deborah as if to say: I know you are his mother or his aunt but this case here is so straightforward that even you, his relative, cannot but agree that I'm right and he is wrong! 'What can I do? Can I pluck out one of my eyes to fix it on the lorry, can I? I tell you I will not. Not even if my master pays me ten pounds a month.'

'You are talking rubbish,' Titus said helplessly. 'Absolute rubbish. You've broken the law.'

'Don't you start abusing me again, I warn you.'

'Let us go now,' Deborah entreated.

The driver continued: 'Yours is not the first car that I have met on this journey. I tell you all the others had not made the bad mistake of thinking that I was a motor-cycle; only amateur drivers cannot tell the sounding of a motor-car engine from that of a motor-cycle's.'

'Do let us go, Titus,' his mother again pleaded. He wasn't getting anywhere. The rascal was unrepentant.

'I want to see your licence,' Titus demanded.

'You don't need to see my licence. Everyone knows my vehicle both in Ibadan and in Lagos. *Safe Journey*. Write it down in your book and go and report me to the police. Who makes you a policeman, anyway?' The man climbed into the driver's seat and started to fumble with its controls.

The crowd that had gathered round both of them persuaded Titus to break up the argument and go his way. The lorry was not a local one and no one knew the driver. One of the men told him that drivers belonged to a breed that did not care for anyone, not even for engineers. Except, of course, the policeman. They feared policemen, with good reason!

Later on that evening a little girl from the Oti household delivered a letter at the vicarage. After reading it a second time the Rev. Morakinyo sent for both Pa Joel and Simeon Oke. To both of them he read out Titus's letter first in English before translating it into Yoruba for the benefit of the old man:

'I am writing to thank you and through you the members of the Harvest Committee for inviting me to open the Bazaar Sales on 27 May next.

'I have given much consideration to this. While appreciating the great honour done me I have reluctantly come to the conclusion that I have to decline it for reasons I shall now endeavour to explain.

'I understand that this role is usually played by an influential member of the Church who usually donates a respectable sum of money, thereby setting a good example for the supporters and the generalty of the church members at the ceremony to follow. The truth is that, as it is only five months since I came back from England, my financial position is still quite bad and I shall be unable to make a donation worthy of a chairman.

'I also consider that it will be better practice not to choose a young man for this role. I respectfully suggest therefore that the Committee should now look round for someone else who in age and affluence and, above all, in Christian piety is more deserving of the honour.

'I enclose herewith a cheque for two guineas as my own contribution to the Bazaar.

'I wish you and your Committee every success.'

After he had translated the letter to Pa Joel, the vicar folded it and put it back in the envelope. He puffed at his pipe.

Pa Joel spoke: 'I do not believe Titus wrote it, Pastor.' He stretched out his hand to Rev. Morakinyo. The latter handed the envelope to the old man. He drew out of it the sheet of paper and purred at it.

Simeon chuckled. 'Why are you staring at the paper as if you can read it? You should say whatever you have to say to this serious matter now that Pastor has read out of the letter from Engineer.'

'It is a very serious matter, Pastor. I do not believe that the son of my nephew Samuel could write those words that you have read to my ear this evening, Pastor. I do not believe it, Pastor.'

'I thought I should bring it to your notice, Elder, and to yours, Brother Simeon, before I summon a meeting of the Harvest Committee.'

All three were silent. Pa Joel's bald head shone in the little light of the kerosene lamp on the table. He coughed preparatory to his next observation: 'These young men! There is no limit to what they will do. Not only has he brought shame to our family and to the memory of his father. He now thinks that he knows better than the members of the Harvest Committee by teaching them how to go about their business. Pastor, is it not every year that we form a Committee to organize the harvest and the Bazaar?'

Pastor Morakinyo puffed at his pipe rapidly and nodded his head rapidly to signify assent.

'Have we not been doing it this way long before Titus was born? It is you I blame for suggesting his name at all.'

'But all the Committee thought that he is the most suitable person,' Simeon said. 'Look, Pa, the important thing is for you to speak to him. He will not refuse you. Speak to him and tell him to reconsider the matter.'

Pastor Morakinyo puffed at his pipe rapidly. He nodded his head rapidly.

'Speak to him? I shall order him to do it. That's what I shall do. He may have been to the white man's country. He may have been to Jerusalem in heaven. He is still Titus. And I am going to tell him that. If he insists on bringing dishonour to the family, and disgrace to the memory of his father, I shall have nothing to do with him. Simeon, we go. And, Pastor, please do not be vexed with him. He is only a small boy. That's what he is. Leave him to me. I shall knock some sense into his head.'

Seven

———◇———

PA JOEL did not succeed in his determination to knock sense into the head of Titus. There were angry scenes between the old man and the young rebel. There were angry scenes between Deborah and her erring son. At each scene between Pa Joel and Titus and between mother and son, Simeon was present; cool, saying little but leaving no doubt as to which side he supported.

But Titus stood his ground. He had paid two guineas towards the Harvest Fund and he was not going to pay a penny extra. As for being the chief opener at the Bazaar he would have nothing whatever to do with it.

After a final family meeting a compromise was announced to the world. Engineer Titus and the whole family appreciated very much the honour done to them by the church congregation in considering Titus suitable for performing the most important function at the Bazaar. Titus had, however, decided to transfer this great honour to the dearly respected head of the family Pa Joel Tobatele. Unfortunately Titus himself would be away, on the day, as he would be having important consultations with the Director of P.W.D. in Lagos. But both his mother, Sister Deborah, and his kinsman, Brother Simeon Oke, would be there to support the head of the family.

There was great excitement in the crowd of gaily dressed women and men dancing to the *shekere* orchestra at the Bazaar. The Pastor and the members of the Harvest Committee sat at a central table flanked on either side by a row of benches on which sat elderly men and women. At the head of the central table was Pa Joel. He was attired in a big *sanyan* suit. On his head was a red cap heavily embroidered. He wore a long gold chain round his neck. The *agbada* of the suit was heavily embroidered round the neck and the chest. His shoes were of a red velvet background on which had been worked some little patterns of flowers in imitation gold. He held in his right hand a horse-tail staff of authority which he waved constantly in greeting to the group of young men and women who danced in the enclosure.

Three of the young women came out to the front and danced in formation. The one in the middle was tall and elegant in her white woollen *buba* and *sanyan iro*. Her brown silk head-tie went very well with her brown sandals. She twisted her waist to the rhythm of the *gangan* drum, the jingling of her gold bangles sounding like part of the music. She danced with her body half-inclined throwing her head from right to left, from left to right, keeping perfect rhythm with the drums.

Simeon Oke came out and pasted two coins on the forehead of each of the dancers to the admiration of all, and the delight of the drummers as the girls after some time passed the coins on to them.

Then Pa Joel got up to dance. The head drummer struck a note which called for silence. Then someone chanted the first line of a song in which they all soon joined:

> Who says we have no father?
> Sure, we have a father.
> Pa Joel is our father.

So who says we have no father,
For sure, we have a father.

The old man might have been moving much or little, it was difficult to tell in the voluminous *sanyan* robe. But happiness radiated from his wrinkled face. He waved the horse-tail to the crowd that applauded his dancing.

Sister Deborah went up to him and, kneeling in greeting to him, got up and pasted one shilling on his forehead. Others of the household and well-wishers followed her example and pasted several shillings and sixpences on the old man's forehead. Then Simeon went up to him. After the old man had, with his free hand, removed the coins from his forehead and handed them to the head drummer Simeon pasted not one or two or three coins but a green ten-shilling note on the old man's forehead. The excitement redoubled when on Simeon's instruction the old man removed the first note and Simeon pasted on another one. And they all danced round him enthusiastically singing:

Who says we have no father?
Sure we have a father.

Soon, Simeon Oke held up both hands and cried for silence. The shout for silence was relayed round the dancing group, the drummers ignoring it for a long time, the dancing women seizing this moment to intensify their dancing, swinging their waists rhythmically from side to side.

When silence of some sort had been achieved Simeon announced that the Chairman, Elder Joel Tobatele, had donated thirty pounds.

'Thirty pounds? What do you say!'

'Thirty pounds! Have you heard old Pa Joel giving thirty pounds! Where did he find it?'

'Where did he find it? What a silly question. Engineer Titus gave it to him of course.'

'Sister Deborah Oti, mother of Engineer Titus Oti has donated – ten pounds,' Simeon again announced.

'Ten pounds, a mere woman!'

'Ten pounds. Sister Deborah has done it in a big way.'

'Thirty pounds from old Joel. And ten from Deborah. That's forty pounds in all. We must salute Engineer Titus. They are fabulously rich in that work they do. When my son leaves this church school I want him to go to the white man's country to study to become what Titus is now.'

After the other supporters had followed the lead of the Chairman and the sale had been going on for some time the crowd had the opportunity they'd been waiting for to see Simeon Oke in action. It was over a tin of cigarettes. Two bidders had reached 7s. 3d. and one of them was already giving up when Simeon shouted 'eight shillings'. This took by surprise the bidder who till then was succeeding. He shouted 'nine shillings'.

'Nineteen shillings,' shouted Simeon.

'One pound,' shouted Pastor Morakinyo!

'One pound ten!' Simeon cried.

'Simeon the Foreman!' The crowd shouted.

Three pounds!' Simeon shouted again without anyone having challenged his bid of one pound ten shillings.

'Simeon! Simeon the Foreman.'

'Five pounds! Five pounds!' he again shouted.

'Simeon, Simeon the tycoon!'

Drawing out from his wallet five red notes, he held them up for the crowd to see. He then gave them to the clerk recording the sales. He opened the tin of cigarettes and took out one. He lit it from a match someone held up for him. He then proceeded to distribute the cigarettes round the crowd.

Smoking, in a sophisticated manner, he began to dance among the group of women dancers. The head drummer beat out a special tune for him. . . .

Simeon the foreman, Simeon the foreman
The man that is money from head to toe
Simeon the foreman, Simeon the foreman
The handsome man beloved of beautiful women
The lion of the P.W.D.
Master of all men that work on the road.
The god that contractors worship.
Simeon the foreman, Simeon the generous man
The one and only elephant
That makes the whole forest tremble when he passes.

Eight

———————◇———————

DURING another of her unannounced early-morning visits two days after the Bazaar, Sister Deborah told Titus of the magnificent performance given by Pa Joel and Simeon at the Bazaar. 'And, Titus, the whole town is talking about the grandeur of it all. They are saying that they have not seen the like of it in the history of our church. Ah! Titus, it brought great glory to our family.'

Titus followed her with interest. Today she had not brought an offending infant, and there was no immediate cause for friction.

'It was grand for Father. Everyone was happy and pleased. He was very pleased and he spent generously.'

'Pa spent money generously – where did he get it from?'

'Everybody said that you gave it to him. And all the church people were full of prayer and praise for you. They pray that when you too become an old man you may have worthy children to support you in your old age. It was very, very glorious, Titus.'

'But, Mother,' he said after a pause. 'I did not give Pa any money. Where did he get the money from?'

'Well, I myself did not believe that you gave him all the money. But I thought you gave him some,' she said

46

looking at him. After some time she continued, 'It must have been your kinsman then that gave him the money. Titus, he was simply splendid.'

'My kinsman the foreman – oh, my God!'

'Titus, why do you speak like that? Has he done something that is not good?'

He did not answer. He lit a cigarette and tried to smoke away his anger.

'Pa sent for you yesterday evening. You did not come. Titus, why I have come now is to find out why you refused to come.'

Still he did not answer. A barrage of cocks crowing came from the neighbouring compound where the Agricultural Officer lived. The barking of his dog in the backyard meant that the dog was aware for the first time that there was a stranger around. Titus had been wondering before why it was that the dog had not barked on her arrival. He sighed at the thought of the many dangers to which she exposed herself by this most inconvenient habit of cockcrow visits. Stepping on a snake in the dark. Murder at the hands of burglars. Attempted rape at the hands of an insane man – God Almighty!

'When your father sends for you, you must come.'

'Mother, you drive me mad. My father is dead. If you mean Pa Joel . . .'

'Yes, I mean him. He is the younger brother of the father of your father. He was therefore your father's father. If he sent for your father when he was alive, wherever he might be and whatever he might be doing, your father would leave it and hurry to him. For he was his father. And so he respected him.'

He sighed at the futility of his effort to show his mother the necessity of distinguishing between the members of a real blood family and those of an extended family. To the white man one's father is the husband of one's mother.

Your brother is the son of your father and of your mother. But to Sister Deborah and all like her the head of the household is father. And there could be many of them in the same family, all living in various areas of the same town or in different villages in the same district: all tracing their origin to one ancestor several generations back; all renewing acquaintance at funerals and at chieftaincy ceremonies.

'Let me tell you the important matter that has brought me this morning. I want you to behave in a better way to your kinsman, Simeon. I want you to act to him with the respect that he deserves.'

Titus was on his guard. 'But, Mother, I'm sick of your talking to me about my kinsman Simeon all the time. Why must you talk of him all the time? Why is he different from all the other relatives we have?'

'He is very different. Very different indeed. He helps us.'

'And is there something at the bottom of all this? If there is I want you to tell me all today. Everything.'

She said stubbornly, 'All I want of you is to give him respect. I treat him with respect. My words are finished.'

'Listen, Mother, tell me something. Just what is it that I do to Simeon that indicates lack of respect? Tell me that.'

'In the first place, why do you call him Simeon? Is he not much older than you? You must call him brother.'

Titus sighed at the hopelessness of the case. 'But he is not my brother. He is not your son, not the son of any of my father's other wives. Therefore he's not my brother.'

'You have been to the white man's country and you know too much. That's the trouble. The man is older than you. He's your brother. And that is all. And, Titus, I know what I'm talking about. Am I a child? Do I not see that you do not respect him? Do I not see that you

48

do not care for him? You must respect him and not shame him in the presence of other people. He has more experience in Government's work than you.'

Thomas came in to tell him that his bath water was ready. He greeted the mother of his master in his imperfect Yoruba and went back to the kitchen.

Titus walked to the window and looked out over the wooded slope. He saw a few women walking happily along the path at the bottom of the slope, balancing baskets and calabashes on their heads and chatting away their woes and the secrets of their husbands. He walked back to his mother and said. 'Mother, I shall tell you something about Simeon my kinsman today. Ever since I came back I've been trying not to mix my private affairs with my work. But you and Pa and the whole lot of you at home have placed me in a very awkward position.'

'What have we done?'

'Simeon my kinsman. That's what you have done. Simeon who, according to all of you, is my kinsman – my brother you call him – is a very bad man.'

'Ah, Titus! You must ask God for forgiveness. Why must you sin against an innocent man. You must pray to God for forgiveness.'

'Simeon is my employee. He is wicked and dishonest.'

'Ah, Titus. Everyone knows that he is very kind. Everyone says so. Pastor too says so. You must be careful not to say this in the presence of Pastor.'

'Pastor and the whole Church think that he is good and kind. That is because he is corrupt. He steals money from his work. He collects money from the labourers whom he employs on the roads.'

'Ah, Titus! How can you say things like this. All his workers like him.'

'So does Pastor, and the whole Church. They like him

because he gives plenty of money to the church building fund. It is all stolen money.'

'Titus, Titus.'

'It is my duty as District Engineer to see that no one steals any money. It is my duty as District Engineer to see that no one collects money from contractors and from workmen. It is therefore my duty to fight my kinsman Simeon and stop him from his evil practices.'

'But, Titus,' she cried in stark horror. 'You cannot fight him. He is very strong. He has plenty of *juju*. My God, I am lost!' She held her breasts. She was visibly distressed.

Nine

———————◇———————

TITUS discovered to his annoyance that his troubles were not confined to the bad relationship between him and his kinsman, the foreman. He received a confidential letter from his Provincial Engineer which made him motor down to the provincial headquarters at Ibadan.

McBain was not pleased to see him – he did not pretend to be. 'The first thing I must impress upon you, Mr Oti, is the necessity to obtain my permission before you leave your station. And—'

'I'm sorry, Mr McBain, but this matter is quite important.'

'That may be so. Nevertheless, before you come to see me, you should arrange an appointment. I might have gone out, perhaps on tour in Ijebu Province as I would have been had I not had to cancel it for an emergency meeting with the Commissioner of Police. In spite of these two lapses on your part, I say a bright good morning to you – do take your seat.'

Titus flushed with anger. Anger at having committed this elementary blunder of not letting the P.E. know that he was coming to see him. He hated being spoken to in this way, particularly on a subject he himself knew very well. Why, he was himself becoming notorious in his office at Ibala for the way in which he would refuse to see anyone who did not first arrange an appointment through his Chief Clerk. There was, for instance, the famous story that he had ordered Pa Joel to wait in the Chief Clerk's Office on one occasion on the excuse that he had no previous appointment with him: and that the old man would have waited there a long, long time had he not decided to defy the messenger and the Chief Clerk and to storm into Titus's office where he had threatened to thrash his erring relative before the Chief Clerk and the messenger intervened and placated the infuriated old man.

'And now to the important matter that has brought you, Mr Oti – cigarette?'

Titus thought he saw a frown on the face of the Scotsman when he thought that he was going to take the only one left in the packet he held towards him. 'Ah, I remember you don't smoke, Mr Oti,' he said, smiling, as he put the packet back in the seat pocket of his khaki shorts.

'It is this letter, Mr McBain,' Titus said, handing him the O.H.M.S. envelope. He took out the sheet from the envelope, and glanced through the contents. He admired his own signature at the bottom.

'Yes, and what about the letter, Mr Oti?'

'What about it? In the first place I'm surprised the lorry had an accident.'

'So are the Police, Mr Oti. And that so soon after your inspection of the lorry, and your certificate of road-worthiness.' The Chief Clerk showed his face through the door and announced that the Resident's Chief Clerk had rung while the P.E. was out and that the Resident would expect the P.E. for golf in the evening.

'Important as that message is, Mr George, I would

prefer your not interrupting me when I'm having an important conference with the District Engineer, Ibala. Well now, Mr Oti?'

'I'm quite surprised at the whole thing. I'm particularly worried at the tone of your letter.'

'The tone of my letter – why?' He asked in surprise. He started to read aloud rapidly the offending letter: 'I have received a report from the Senior Superintendent of Police, Central Area, that Bedford lorry Registered No. PL 459 was involved in a serious accident on the Iperu–Abeokuta Road on 16 May last. Seven people were killed and thirteen others seriously injured. The letter from the Police also contained the information that their inspection of the lorry after the accident revealed that a great many of its parts were mechanically defective. The Police finally said that the lorry was inspected by you and issued with a roadworthiness certificate only seven days before the accident. You are required to let me have as a matter of urgency your report on this rather serious matter.'

He looked up at Titus after reading the letter he had himself written and signed. 'Well, Mr Oti, what particularly worries you about this letter?'

'The tone, as I have said; you wrote as if you already believe that I committed a crime.' He looked the other man straight in the face.

'Nothing of the sort, my dear man.' McBain sighed philosophically. 'As Provincial Engineer it is my duty to do very little believing in the things I'm told in this blessed job. I've no more than passed on to you an allegation that I have received about our Department. It is from the head of another Department of Government. When you are a little older in the Civil Service you will learn the wisdom of never allowing the ball to remain dead in your own half of the field. You play it first to your immediate subordinate. When he plays it back to you – assuming he is not a fool, or an imbecile – you play it vertically up to your immediate superior if the query originated from above, or sideways to whoever originated it if it was outside your Department. A game of musical chairs, if you like to look at it another way. The man without a chair when the music stops loses, Mr Oti.'

'I see,' Titus said.

'All I want you to do is to write back to me your own side of the story. Surely you have your own side. No, don't explain it to me now. It must be in writing – everything in writing. This I shall incorporate in another letter. It will, in fact, be your own letter endorsed to the Police, see? You do not look like a criminal thirsting for blood. Even if you are, I am sure you will think of a neater method of covering your tracks than certifying a defective lorry as perfect. And I let you into a secret, Mr Oti,' he regarded him for some time before proceeding. 'Old Kennedy, the S.S.P., does not care as much for road safety as he pretends. I know that for certain, Mr Oti.'

'I certainly shall write all that I know about that lorry. It was perfectly all right when I tested it.'

'Good; and by the way, I have not seen your Form 195 in respect of expenditure on the District Roads for the month of May. We've got to have these figures. Without them we cannot compile our own records for the returns to headquarters. I've already signed a letter of query to you, Mr Oti. Don't be disturbed when you get it. You clear your court by promptly sending a suitable reason for your delay. And, of course, you send in your Form 195, duly completed and signed by you. Matter of routine, see, Mr Oti?'

Titus stopped for a glass of beer and relaxation at the

All Races Club. He was not yet a member and was not entitled to go in there without being introduced by a member. But no one observed this rule which he himself did not know.

It was there at the club that he encountered her again, the girl he had first met in hardly friendly circumstances at the Post Office, the girl who had attended the memorial and thanksgiving festivities at Ibala and had immediately afterwards disappeared before he came to know her well. She wore a green up-and-down attire, with green silk head-tie and white buckled sandals. Titus did not know the solitary person on one of the high stools at the bar and so he walked with steady steps to the table where the girl sat alone. He surprised himself at the speed with which he went into the attack. Would she have a glass of beer? No, whisky and soda.

'Steward, whisky and soda for the lady. One squash for me please.' She did not appear to think it strange or unusual that a stranger had ordered a drink for her. When it came, she drank it quietly, but fast.

Would she have another? Yes, she would!

He asked her her name. She told him it was Bimpe. But the boys called her Bimp – Auntie Bimp. She said she remembered having seen him more than once before. He reminded her of the Post Office incident, and of her attendance at the service at Ibala. She smiled in embarrassment as she said that she remembered both occasions. She knew he was a stranger in town as she had not met him at the All Races Club or at any of the other bars in Ibadan.

'Another whisky and soda, Miss—?'

'Auntie Bimp. You have my permission to call me so. That's what all the boys call me.'

'Another whisky and soda, Auntie Bimp?' He said the name with an affectionate explosion on the last syllable.

He knew he was at the beginning of an adventure. He needed one.

'No, not yet, my dear.'

'Or just beer, then?'

'Stout. When I'm ready I'll tell you. But order something for yourself,' she said, looking at his empty glass. They both saw that it wasn't quite empty. Two flies appeared to find the limited space inside the glass ideal for what appeared to be romance in their particular part of the insect world. He called the steward and ordered a repeat of the squash. She laughed softly.

'And what makes you laugh so much, if I may ask?' he asked softly. She laughed again and explained that she knew that some men only drank soft drinks and that she had learnt not to trust them as such men usually made up for it in other directions.

He ordered lunch.

He looked through the window. He showed interest in a car in the limited grounds of the club. An old black Ford Prefect, registration No. CL 457. He thought the number ticked.

She followed his interest in the car and said, 'Foreman Simeon's car. *Alakori*. The man is not serious at all.'

'Oh yes?'

'That car has been there for well over two months. He has—'

'Two months!' Titus exclaimed.

Definitely up to two months. You don't know Foreman Simeon. When he is drunk he can drive his car anywhere and abandon it there. . . . He left it here this time after the dance of the last Muslim Festival. He had promised to take me back home. Had I not made alternative arrangements I would have been stranded. He did not even know with whom I went eventually – he was much too tight.' He was listening to her only absent-mindedly. He was pondering the fact that only the day before he had approved the papers of the foreman for his mileage allowance for the month of May in respect of Ford Prefect saloon CL 457! He had claimed to have done 1,487 miles in that month. He always claimed a heavy mileage every month. Now the District Engineer was with his own eyes seeing CL 457 rotting away at the All Races.

'You know the Foreman then?'

'Know the Foreman?' she repeated, as if she could not believe that he need ask her this.

'Your husband?' he risked the question.

'Husband! Oh no.'

Both of them looked up as the steward brought two plates of rice with soup and meat. They watched him put the plates down, smooth out the creases in the not-so-clean table-cloth, and make an unnecessary adjustment to the knives and forks in front of Titus.

'Live with Foreman Simeon!' she sighed as she handed the salt to him. 'Impossible. Not with that third wife of his – that wretched girl from Lagos. She's been thrown out by one man after another in Lagos and Ibadan. She's gone to dump herself in Simeon's house. She thinks everyone is like her, thinking that I want to steal her husband from her. She is a great *juju* woman – she knows *juju malams* in Ibadan and Ibala.'

'Oh yes?' he managed to say, trying to cool a spoonful of rice that was burning the inside of his mouth.

'I am the only child of my mother. I promised her that I will not die young. I run away from *juju* women.'

They both concentrated on the food for a moment. He drank some water and looked at her inquiringly. She understood, and said that she couldn't mix stout with rice. He was relieved.

He asked after some pause: 'What is your work?'

'I am a lady contractor.'

'A lady contractor?' he echoed. He wondered immediately why she had not visited him at Ibala. There were
two other women who he'd chased out of his office at
Ibala. They were not attractive and they had nothing else
to recommend them. This one was more than attractive.
Above all, she knew the Foreman and could have used
her position with him and her attractiveness to an
embarrassing extent.

'And how's work?'

'Not too bad. That's the one thing I must praise
Foreman Simeon for. He gives me plenty of work. I'm
going to see him at Ibala on Friday. He gave me a
requisition for two hundred yards of laterite. I'm chasing
the lorry driver and the labourers. If I don't, they'll
cheat me.' She was silent for some time, then she said
pushing away the plate, 'the rice is no good. I've told the
manager to sack this cook – he won't.'

'Why don't I see you when you come to Ibala?'

'I always see you. I sent Foreman Simeon to you. He
tells me that you don't like to be seen with women in the
office.'

There was an embarrassing silence after this, mercifully
ended by a boisterous shout from someone just coming
in 'Titus Oti, can this be true?'

'Chris Daniels, by all that is wonderful!'

'Titus, whatever are you doing here?'

'Oh, having lunch.'

'And making love to Auntie Bimp. You fellows from
Ibala are fast. You come to town for half a day and steal
the most beautiful women. Steward, whisky and soda
for the District Engineer of Ibala.'

'No. Orange squash.'

'You are still the same, then. I hope you know who he
is, Auntie? He is the most important person in the

P.W.D. He is going to be the first African Director of P.W.D.'

Auntie Bimp smiled coquettishly.

'He will give you all the contracts, Auntie. You just stay on the right side of him. Here's your squash, Titus. I haven't seen you since that dance at the International Friendship League at Leicester Square, last year. You said you were going home four days after.'

'I did.'

'I came back four months ago myself.'

'How's the work?'

'Mustn't complain. But the fact is that there are far too many lawyers sitting here. They just rush here from Lagos. I'm rather worried, to be frank. But, one mustn't complain. Auntie, another whisky and soda?'

'Lawyer, I've already had three.'

'Then have a fourth.'

'You lawyers deceive people by saying that you have no money. D.E., don't believe them. They ride in big cars and complain that they have no money.'

'You must believe me, Auntie. I must ride in a Pontiac to keep up appearances. Otherwise I won't impress my clients. But when they see me in a big car and decent suits, they think I'm important and clever, and will impress the judge. Now you know the secret of the big car, Auntie. Will you do me the honour of riding in it tonight. Or has the District Engineer already forestalled me?'

'Oh, I'm going back to Ibala in the next half an hour.'

'By the way I've sent a petition to you, old boy. My client has been served with a contravention notice by your people. Something to do with building too near the road. He says your people and the sanitary inspector all saw the building when he first set it out. They had no objection. He'd satisfied their requirements. Now when he was nearly completing the house you came on inspection and told him to demolish it.'

'He has contravened the Building Line Ordinance. I remember the case well. At Iwana, wasn't it?'

'Yes, Iwana.'

'Instead of seventy-five feet from the centre line of the road, he's only forty-five.'

'But your people allowed him to start. You should overlook it, man. If you don't you'll have several such cases on your hand. What can you do? If you go to court we are sure to get judgement against you. And the man is good, when you come to know him, Titus.'

'I'm sure he's good. He tried to bribe me.'

'No. He told me that you refused to allow him to see you at home. I do not want you to encourage these people to come to your house; you know what I mean. But my client is good. He knows people that matter in Ibala. Look, Titus, I want you to withdraw the contravention notice.'

On the way back to Ibala Titus reflected on his problems. The problem of the lorry accident in which his professional name was involved and the theory of Mr McBain about this merely acting as a Post Office. The discovery of yet another of Simeon's frauds, the car that was off the road. The problem of the sinner against the Building Line Ordinance and of Chris his lawyer friend who, because of his twenty-guinea fees, wanted him to overlook the matter – what did he care whether or not the proposed development marred the orderly growth of the town for generations to come? As to Auntie Bimp he knew he was embarking upon an adventure of a complicated kind.

Ten

———————◇———————

Two days after Titus visited Ibadan, Bimpe called at his office at Ibala, accompanied by Barrister Christopher Daniels. The messenger had used his discretion and let in the smartly-dressed woman and the man without first asking them their names and going through the usual formalities.

'Good morning, sir,' she said sweeping into the room. 'I told you I would come, and now I've come.'

Chris hung round her like a waiter.

'Good morning, Auntie Bimp. You're certainly welcome. And you too, Chris. I apologize for the bareness of my office. A reflection on the financial situation of our Government.' Titus noticed that today he was not as brave and daring as he had been with the woman two days before at Ibadan.

'And what brings you here, Chris?'

'Business. Business of earning my daily bread, my boy.'

'We seldom see you men of the learned profession this way. This must be a special occasion.'

The room was full of scent. Bimpe crossed her legs where she sat, her blue damask *iro* over white lace *buba* rustling as she did so. She took a fan with a nude picture on it out of her handbag, dropped the bag in his in-tray, and proceeded to do her head-tie again. Titus noticed that her eyes roved round the room. He understood.

'I'm sorry I have no mirror in here, Auntie Bimp.'

'You must have one installed, man,' Chris said looking round the walls. 'And about time you replaced a few of these maps and charts with pin-ups. Auntie Bimp will this morning give you one of her best portraits. It will do well up there—'

'Lawyer!' She cried, bringing out a blue compact from her handbag and using its tiny mirror to direct her operation of doing the head-tie. 'I shall give D.E. a photo. But not till he's put up Bola's photo.'

Titus was startled. Just how did she know about Bola?

'D.E., I told you I was coming to see you. I have fulfilled my promise.'

'And have I not welcomed you, Auntie Bimp. And to remove any shadow of doubt – welcome again to you, Auntie Bimp!' He tried to put as much gallantry as he could into it.

Chris laughed.

'You have not asked what I've come for, D.E.' she said, studying her polished finger-nails.

'And what can I do for you, miss?'

'Everything. And you must promise to do everything I ask – but, Lawyer, why don't you sit down? When you are not pleading before the Magistrate I think you should sit down.'

Chris came away from the maps and charts he'd been studying and sat down.

'D.E., I want you to give me contracts,' Bimpe said looking at Titus coyly.

'Contracts. And that's why you've come all the way from Ibadan?'

'Is it not important enough? It is a very, very important thing for me. For you it is a very, very small thing. Therefore you will do it for me very easily.'

The telephone rang.

'District Engineer . . . Yes . . . who? Oh no. You have to go to Ibadan for that I'm afraid . . . where in Ibadan? At the headquarters. When you get to the Secretariat at Agodi, ask for the P.W.D. Headquarters. Yes, bye-bye.' And he rang off.

'You've come for contracts,' he said, trying to remember the point where the conversation had been broken off by the telephone interruption. 'And I see you've brought your solicitor along too. To advise on the transaction eh?' He thought he should draw Chris into the conversation.

'What, me?' Chris swallowed the bait. 'Why, you must know that I merely gave Auntie Bimp a lift, please. I am no more than hers and your obedient servant. You see before you here the most harmless male in the country. Aunti Bimp herself has seen to that when she married me to her younger sister.'

'I thought you'd come along to prepare the contract agreement. Supply of fifty cubic yards of gravel at five and sixpence a yard. Contract sum, thirteen pounds fifteen shillings. Lawyer's fees, ten pounds!'

'Ten guineas. We go in guineas, not pounds,' Chris corrected and explained. 'But knowing Auntie as a close relative I shall reduce my fees to eight guineas – have a cigarette, Titus,' he said holding a smart cigarette-case out to him.

'Thank you, man. I'm a bad host,' he said, selecting a cigarette. 'I ought to have offered you one myself.'

'That's okay by me,' Chris said, extending the case to

Bimpe. She took one. Chris went on as he held the lighter to the cigarette for her. 'When we come to the next round and to the round after that, you can be sure we shall deplete your stock.'

The telephone rang again.

'District Engineer. Who? Ah, Ian McLapperton. You here in Ibala? Marvellous. Most welcome. As a matter of fact I have a lady with me now together with her solicitor! Going through to see the Ibala Grammar School Project? I really don't need to come. You'll find the foreman around, I hope. That's fine. I tell you what, Ian, why not drop in on your way back and have a glass of beer? That will be grand. Any time, between four and five. Good-bye.'

Bimpe blew a ring of blue smoke. She knocked off the ash from the cigarette end. 'Lawyer is already impatient,' she said. 'He wants to run away. But the magistrate isn't here yet.'

'Are you going to abandon her to me?'

'Look, man, I'm dead serious when I say that I have no interest in Auntie Bimp, in that way. The field is completely clear for you as I see it. You must believe what I say. Not that Auntie Bimp is not charming. All Ibadan worships at her shrine – and I now see the religion has spread to Ibala here.'

'Lawyer! Go on with your flattering.' But Auntie Bimp was pleased.

'And not that I'm insensitive to female charms, either, I confess. Particularly when the charmer is of the calibre of Auntie Bimp here.'

'Lawyer! Lawyer!'

'Nor am I an angel. Mother tried her best to make me one. I just wasn't made to be one. Now that Auntie has arranged to marry me to her younger sister – she's made me harmless. There's somewhere in the Book of

64

Common Prayer, I believe, where the Church of God invokes the wrath of God upon any Christian man who marries the sister of his wife. See my disability?'

'But you are not a Christian, Chris, in spite of your name.'

'And, Lawyer, you have not yet given my sister a wedding ring. It's a shame that she had to pay for the ring she now wears herself. It was done for her by my own goldsmith. I know what she paid for it.'

'Ah, I've got to go now,' Chris said, getting up. 'That's my clerk beckoning to me. Apparently the Magistrate has arrived. I must now go to worship at the altar of His Worship.'

After Chris had left, Titus offered her a cigarette. He was conscious of the wide margin between the lawyer's silver case and the plain tin case from which he now offered her his own cigarette. It was the same brand and must have tasted the same though.

'How do you get back to Ibadan today?' he asked her.

'Lawyer will take me back. And if I like I may go back with the Magistrate himself. I'm Auntie to all of them, my dear.'

They were both silent for a moment. He almost wished she would go so that he might get some work done. He'd completely lost the trend of the report on the flooding at the airport, which he was on when the visitors had arrived. He liked her company. But he wanted to get on with his work.

She broke the silence: 'Or if you give me a contract now I can stay here in Ibala to organize it.'

'With the Foreman, I imagine,' he said, managing to hide the sarcasm.

'I do not stay with Foreman Simeon; I've told you I cannot stick his wives, particularly the third one, that one that has come to dump herself on him here in Ibala. She believes very much in *juju*. As I've told you, there is no *juju malam* in Ibadan or Lagos that she does not know. Look, D.E., I beg you not to eat in the house of any woman – don't let them put love-potions in your food. They may poison you that way.' She seemed to be genuinely concerned for his safety. 'And now which contract are you going to give me today?'

He sighed. He looked at her but said nothing.

'Are you going to call the Chief Clerk to prepare the contract requisition?' she asked in earnest.

'Look, Auntie Bimp. You embarrass me. You tell me you are a contractor, just what do you know about contracting?'

She appeared surprised. 'Why do you ask me this question, D.E.? I have been doing contract work for over three years.'

'Honestly, what do you know about the difference between clean, sharp sand free from salt and deleterious matter, and dirty sand? What do you know about the difference between good laterite and bad laterite?'

'Why do you ask me questions as if I'm a child?' she appeared hurt. 'It is my fault—'

'I don't want you to feel hurt. But this is business. We must cast sentiments and emotions aside, and face the issue seriously. Have you ever heard of the Nigerian Public Works Specifications? What do you know about reinforced concrete? About concrete mixes, about concrete placing?'

She was quite hurt, and angry. She cried out in defence, 'Do you say I don't know about concrete? I tell you I supervised the house of Foreman Simeon at Ibadan. I saw the contractor put in the right amount of concrete. You think only engineers know these things? I tell you you are mistaken, D.E.' She was quite hurt. He saw it.

66

'You know all about concrete. Tell me, Contractor, how did you measure the concrete you used in the staircase?'

'I shall tell you, then you will see that I know what I'm talking about. We first measured two headpans of gravel. Then we measured two headpans of sand. Then we added two headpans of cement. Then we added two headpans of water. You still say I don't know?'

The Engineer chuckled. 'You mean you had equal measures of stone, sand and cement. That must be extraordinary. Incidentally, you have not mentioned the amount of steel reinforcement you placed in the staircase.'

'Steel reinforcement – what's that?'

'Rods. Iron rods.'

'Ah, iron rods. I must confess that I don't remember how many we put in now. But there were plenty. Maybe sixty or so. And that's why the staircase is so strong. And the whole house is very strong. Look, D.E., I don't see why you are *lawyering* me as if you are a lawyer pleading before a Magistrate. I do not like it at all. All I want from you is contract work. I knew you properly only a few days ago and you begin to *lawyer* me like this.'

'I'm sorry. Very sorry.'

'If you give me contract work, I will do it well. And if you give me a big contract like a bridge construction—'

'Bridge construction, good Lord!'

'Yes, bridge construction, why not? If you give it to me I can get someone to help me do it. When Foreman Simeon gave me six miles of road construction in Ibala–Iwana Road last year there were many culverts. His men constructed the road. And the men of the Yard Superintendent constructed the culverts.'

'Good Lord, I see!'

'And I paid them all very well. That's how we do it. And if you give me a big job, that's how we are going to do it. You, too, will help make all the arrangements. Won't you give me another cigarette, dear?'

Eleven

———————◇———————

Two days later, Titus received a note from Bimpe informing him that she was in town and would like to see him at Elder Matthew's as soon as he could make it after office hours. It was written in a characteristic feminine hand, and it brought back memories of the days when he and Bola courted each other. Curiously enough Bimpe's writing was remarkably like Bola's. But her English was poor. He had guessed for some time that she could not have gone far in formal education and was most unlikely to have had any secondary school education at all. Girls of her type never settled down to much schooling.

What business would she be having with Elder Matthew? He wondered. He remembered that the old man had complained to Pa Joel and to Sister Deborah that since Titus came back from the white man's country he had not done him the honour of calling to see him in his house. Yet, the old man bragged, so many important people from Ibala and Ibadan and indeed Lagos came to see him. He had not wanted anything from Titus but to pray for him, in his work. Titus considered that this day of Bimpe's visit was as good as any for paying off the old man's debt.

He knew Pa Matthew's house and remembered that, as in most houses in Ibala, the external door led into a corridor flanked on both sides by rooms. In the corridor he was told that Elder Matthew was busy having a meeting but that Bimpe had left word that if he called he should be brought to the back of the house where she would be expecting him. He followed his guide through the corridor to the back-yard – and into the world of the Prophets of Ibala. There were many people there, and as is usual at church services and other religious gatherings there were more women than men. They were arranged in three rows, the women filling two and the men one row of benches. He saw that while the majority of them were sitting down a number of them were kneeling. He would have retreated except that the sitting arrangement was such that by now everyone had caught sight of him and retreat had become impossible.

He heard someone ring a hand-bell of the type that was a common feature on the table of the headmaster of every elementary school. It was Elder Matthew. He wore a long white *kaftan* and a red cap. Then someone cried 'Allelu—'

'Allelujah!' the whole crowd shouted.

'Allelu—'

'Allelujah!'

'Allelu!'

'Allelujah!'

Elder Matthew beckoned to him. He moved towards him mechanically and sat on a chair that someone had quickly placed next to the old man's at the High Table. Then the Elder launched forth into a speech. He called on the congregation to look on that meeting as a very special one. For they were all living witnesses to the work of the Lord who had himself guided the footsteps of their august visitor, Engineer Titus Oti, to the house of prayer and of prophecy. They must all count it a great honour that he had been led to join them and they should pray that from that time on he would continue to meet with them and to participate in their prayers and praises to the Lord God of Hosts. In the name of the congregation he welcomed the august visitor.

'Allelu—'

'Allelujah!'

'Allelu—'

'Allelujah!'

'Allelu—'

'Allelujah!'

Then a woman's voice raised a popular song in Yoruba, in which the whole congregation joined, accompanied by a band of three drums and an empty beer bottle from which a little boy produced an excellent rhythm with a four-inch nail.

'I am a son of God, Allelujah,

'I am a son of God, Allelujah,

'The Devil can do nothing with me for

'I am a son of God, Allelujah.'

They were now all on their feet – and he noticed for the first time that they were all barefooted. They all sang at the top of their voices. They clapped their hands and swayed their hips in unison with the rhythm.

The effect on Titus was tremendous. This was a religious song with a difference. It produced in him a completely different effect from the prayers and responses at the services at All Souls which were sung in a tediously monotonous manner. It was entirely different from the effect produced on him by Pastor Morakinyo singing in a single musical note the three prayers after the creed. This was worship in a true African setting. And mechanically he removed his own shoes and joined in the singing and the clapping of hands.

He had seen Bimpe during Elder Matthew's speech of welcome. She sat at the end of the second bench of the middle row. She wore a white linen *buba* and an *iro* and head-tie of the same material. She had smiled recognition at him, but in his place of honour at the side of Elder Matthew he had acknowledged this only by a slight nod of the head so that he might not attract too much attention to the true and original purpose of his visit.

The song which was only four lines long took several minutes to sing. As one set of people were finishing the last line another set would start the first line. And when it appeared that the whole congregation were guiding themselves to a stop someone from the first row would revive the whole thing and the whole congregation would burst forth with renewed energy.

They were at various points on the third line when someone shouted 'Allelujah!' It was certainly called out of place and Titus looked in the direction where the shout had come. Others, more familiar with the proceedings at these prayer meetings, did not allow this trite incident to distract their attention from the song they were singing. After all, what other word in the whole church vocabulary was more shouted in the course of a service than Allelujah! It was the shout of joy and of victory, the shout of salvation and of redemption.

But even the most devout worshippers showed some concern when a few moments later the same individual again shouted 'Allelujah.' It was equally misplaced, and this time he appeared to be in pain. As they all looked at him they saw that his eyes were dilated. Suddenly the hymn-book he was holding fell out of his hands and he fell forward heavily across the bench.

People in the immediate vicinity of the stricken brother showed more concern for their own safety than for the man lying prostrate before them. In a very short time his bench was deserted. A woman cried in terror and took to her heels. But it must be said to the credit of the core of worshippers that they continued their singing as if they were disgusted with comrades of so little faith that were making so much fuss about such a little incident.

Elder Matthew rose to speak, and to give direction to the thought and activities of the congregation, more and more of whom appeared to be getting confused. He shouted the magic word Allelujah three times, and it was repeated after him three times. 'My brethren and sisters in the faith,' he began. 'Do not allow yourselves to be shaken in your faith and in your worship by this occurrence. Do not be unduly worried about the fate of this our brother in salvation. Do not show undue concern for his body. It is about the soul of Bandele that we must show anxiety. For his body is no more than earth – mere earth. And we have faith in the Lord our Saviour that he has received salvation regardless of what happens to his body – Allelujah.'

'Allelujah.'

'This is an occasion for joy and thanks to the great Jehovah that he has not counted this our brother a mere worker in the P.W.D. unworthy of the great divine message that He wishes to communicate to us His children. He is without doubt a sinner, a great sinner. But when our Saviour first came to the world did he seek the sinner or the holy? Are we all here not sinners? Am I not a sinner? are you not a sinner? But I ask you all, brethren in the faith, was there a greater sinner than Saul of Tarsus? But did Saul in all his sin not receive salvation? The same Lord that washed Saul clean of his sin and made him become Paul the greatest of the apostles has cleansed all of us of our sins and extended to all of us His salvation, Allelujah.'

'Allelujah!'

'The selection of our brother here for this great divine message is the greatest evidence that we in our little congregation here have seen salvation. The divine message is much too great for his body, which is mere earth. That is why he fell down senseless before the Lord his Maker. Let all of us assist him with our prayers that the Devil may not overcome him, that he might be restored back to health that he might deliver to us His great message.

'Allelu—'

'Allelujah!'

'Allelu—'

'Allelujah!'

'Allelu—'

'Allelujah!'

And the whole host went down on their knees. They all said their prayers each completely unmindful of the presence of the others. So many people saying so many different things about the same thing in the same room and at the same time – it was an experience better experienced than imagined. And Titus imagined that only God to whom these supplications were addressed could have made anything of it all. He tried to listen to a man next to him. He thought his whole attitude was more that of someone demanding a right and not begging a favour. This petitioner reminded the Lord of the several promises He had made in the scriptures that whenever they His children prayed, their prayers would be granted. He was therefore calling on the Lord to make good His promises. He should not allow Satan to triumph, which would be the case should the stricken brother not survive the visitation that he might deliver the important message to the rest of the congregation. This man went on in this vein until a female voice started the first line of a popular hymn of praise in Yoruba. This warned the worshippers to wind up their prayers and to join in the singing at various stages in the first verse.

Titus took stock of the extraordinary situation around him. It suddenly occurred to him that the stricken Bandele might die unless he received medical aid, if only to supplement the spiritual aid which the congregation were busily administering on their knees. If he died there would certainly be all sorts of complications, like police investigations and reports, a post-mortem and a coroner's inquest. Someone might want to know how much effort he, an enlightened person, had made to get the patient to the hospital. He knew at the same time, that to touch the stricken man would be nothing short of desecration and would earn him the condemnation of all the worshippers. He got up and, unmindful of what Elder Matthew thought of him, hurried out of the place. He drove straight to his office and phoned to the hospital. The doctor was in, but it was operation day and he was in the middle of a major operation during which he could not be disturbed. The nursing sister said she would go in the ambulance to see what she could do. The police inspector told him that he was used to the prophets of Elder Matthew's fold seeing visions, that not one in his experience had died in the act, and that the District Engineer should not be upset by what he had witnessed.

As he was stopping outside Matthew's house on his return he saw Bimpe standing outside. She came down the verandah. He held open the door for her and she climbed into the car.

'Is he dead?' he asked, as he started to drive away.

'Dead? Of course not,' she answered, surprised.

75

'Survived his visitation? Most wonderful.'

'But why shouldn't he, D.E.?' she asked. 'Were you expecting him to die, then?'

'No, of course not,' he muttered.

'Yes. He has come round. And delivered his prophecy.'

'Ah, so Bandele is now a prophet. What exactly has he prophesied now, Auntie Bimp?' he asked, unable to keep the sarcasm out of his voice. 'More money for contractors, with less work?'

'He has seen a vision of the end of the world,' she said rather slowly.

'The end of the world,' he repeated meditatively as he negotiated a sharp corner. 'But this has been coming for nearly two thousand years. Surely it does not require a road-section man to remind the world that every twenty-four hours mankind is one step nearer Judgement Day.'

'But, D.E., the vision of Bandele is quite genuine. And I don't want you to take it lightly. I've always known Bandele is a holy man.'

'But, my dear Auntie Bimp, are you suggesting for a moment that Bandele is a greater Prophet than all those in the Bible, or a greater authority on the subject of the Day of Judgement being at hand? Did Jesus himself not preach the nearness of it nearly two thousand years ago?'

They were both silent for a moment as he manoeuvred the car towards his house. Then she said slowly. 'D.E., somehow I think you are mistaken in your attitude about Bandele's vision. I want you to take it seriously. And I want you to come to the prayer meetings at Elder Matthew's place.'

'Just why?'

'Because the Day of Judgement is near?'

'And is that the only reason why I should attend the

prayer meetings, Auntie Bimp?' he looked her straight in the face and in that act broke the fundamental rules of road safety.

'There certainly is another reason, my dear,' she said. 'I want you to.'

Twelve

————————◇————————

RETURNING from inspecting a new bridge construction
on the Ibala–Iwana Road, Titus drove absent-mindedly
into the P.W.D. yard. He had noticed, to his dismay,
that the Obalola contravention at Iwana had progressed
considerably, and he was preoccupied with drafting in
his mind an instruction about it to the foreman. He
applied the foot-brake hard and managed, only by inches,
to avoid running into the rear of an enormous Pontiac.
He swore in a manner characteristic of his profession. The
car was neatly though tightly parked in his own garage.
He recognized it quickly enough as belonging to Christopher Daniels. What was he doing in Ibala again so
soon?

He acknowledged half-heartedly the cumbersome
greetings of petty contractors who watched his coming
in and going out. They greeted him in traditional Yoruba
fashion. How was madam? How was the whole household?

Two doors from his room Titus sniffed the air. Scent,
without doubt. Bimpe was with Chris.

'Chris, Chris,' he said addressing Chris and looking
away from Bimpe. 'I wasn't aware you were coming
today. You've not been waiting long, I hope?'

'Not too long. But first things first,' Chris said, 'Ladies first. Even though you are only a bush engineer you must have heard that before. I must insist therefore that you pay your respects to the one and only – Auntie Bimp.'

'Lawyer, leave me and D.E. alone. We know each other.'

'Good morning, Auntie Bimp. Forgive my manners.'

'I shall be your advocate in this case. Your Worship, my client lives in the wilds of Ibala where ladies-of-the-soil are nil and where visiting beauties come only very, very occasionally. I therefore respectfully request Your Worship to overlook my client's seemingly bad manners. I assure Your Worship that they are wholly unintentional.'

'Lawyer!' she laughed.

'May I remind Your Worship that in court language that would be said thus: "I accept the submission of Defence Counsel. Counsel may proceed."'

They all laughed. Titus had sat down. He frowned at a note on his desk. 'Excuse me a moment,' he said. 'I'm asked to ring the Superintendent of Police. Operator, please give me Two-seven. Two-seven – seven; one, two three, four, five six, seven. Yes Two-seven. My number is One-three. That's right.'

'Court again, Chris?' he asked as he put down the receiver. 'I didn't know the Magistrate was sitting here this week.'

'Right, my boy. He isn't. I've come to see a client of mine. We who do not have a regular income have to work hard, driving thousands of miles to make ends meet.'

'I wouldn't mind driving several thousand miles in that limousine of yours,' Titus retorted. 'I see you've crowded me out of my garage.'

'D.E., I want you to buy one like that. Lawyer, I want

you to order one like that for D.E.' Bimpe looked at him. He thought he really liked her. She read his mind as she said: 'D.E. I've asked Lawyer to order one car like his for you. That will fit your dignity as D.E.'

'Where am I to find the money?'

'Money? You mustn't talk like that. You will find the money. And you will find so much money that you will "dash" me your present car. Then I shall use it for supervising the contracts which you will give me.'

'Titus, old boy. I think I must be leaving now. Auntie is safe with you.'

'I'm safe with her, you mean,' he said.

'Lawyer, you can't go like that,' she said. 'First of all give me a few cigarettes. I have been expecting D.E. to offer me some, but he doesn't seem to want to.'

Both of them offered her cigarettes. She preferred to take one from Titus's less elegant case.

'Before you go, Lawyer, we must discuss this important matter with D.E.'

Chris asked, 'Contracts? I've told you that when you reach the appropriate stage you should call me. I shall prepare the proper agreement with all the legal trimmings: "Whereas Mr Titus Oti, District Engineer of the Department of Public Works, Ibala, of the first part. . . . And whereas Madam Bimpe Alagbaja, popularly known as Auntie Bimp, of the other part . . ." '

The telephone rang. 'Yes, District Engineer here. Yes, Yes. Who's speaking? St David's College? Yes, do you want me? No, I didn't ring you at all. Three-seven d'you say? Oh well, I asked the Operator for Two-seven. He's a nuisance. Sorry.'

'D.E., I don't come for contracts today. At least not primarily. It's another very important matter I come for. I do not want you to transfer Foreman Simeon away from Ibala.'

'Transfer the Foreman from Ibala?' he repeated. 'Whatever are you talking about?'

'I don't want you to transfer him from here. Please let him continue here. Don't talk yet. Promise you will do it as a favour for me. D'you promise, dear?' She became quite enchanting.

But his utter lack of comprehension of what she was saying made her charm pass unnoticed.

'Who's transferring Simeon, anyway?' he asked.

'When you talk like that you pretend as if you don't know he's to go to the Cameroons.'

'Cameroons – my God!'

'Didn't you arrange it, D.E.?'

Titus looked at her and shook his head slowly. He said: 'I know absolutely nothing about it.'

Chris spoke: 'You see, Auntie Bimp. Didn't I tell you it couldn't be true? I'm sure Titus knows nothing about it. I know the rumour is all over the place that he has persuaded the Provincial Engineer to arrange the transfer. As I told you on the way here, Titus is not the kind of man that would do a thing like that. Not to Uncle Simeon. Apparently he knows absolutely nothing about the whole affair.'

'Absolutely nothing, I assure you, Chris. The whole thing is ridiculous. Honestly I know nothing about the fellow being transferred. In any case why are you interested in the question of his transfer?'

'Titus, the fellow's a great chap. You here at Ibala don't know his worth. Case of a prophet having no honour in his own town. He's a pillar of the Club – All Races, I mean. A committee member. In spite of his being based at Ibala he does more for the Club than any other member of the Committee at Ibadan.'

'I see.'

'And a most jovial fellow, a great mixer. Whoever is

thinking of his transfer must stop it. Otherwise he'll have the blood of the Club upon his head. Look, I'll take one of your cigarettes, and then disappear round the corner.'

After both his visitors had left him the question of the transfer of Simeon came into his thoughts again and again. He had not thought of it, but curiously enough it would have been a most neat solution to an irritating problem. Apparently – if a transfer to a good distance off were possible – the wretched man's friends would rally round him and, of course, he too would put up a fight. But it was an attractive thought.

Late in the evening of the day after Bimpe's visit he received the first indication of the type of fight his kinsman was putting up. He got a letter from his great uncle, Pa Joel.

'My dear son,' it started. 'It is with much gladness and peace that I write this letter to you. I hope it will find you in peace and in health, as I am here today. We are all well and happy here at home, and everyone here at home sends greetings to you.

'There is an important thing that has made me write this letter to you. I want to tell you that you have offended me. You have not given me the respect you ought to give to me as your father. For after Oti the father of Samuel your father was born, I was born. I am, therefore, your father and you ought to give me much respect. But since you came back from the white man's Country you have not given me respect. You do not give me money regularly. You know I am an old man now. When a rodent becomes old does it not suckle from the breasts of its offspring? You must support me and send me money regularly. Then I shall pray for you as Isaac prayed for Jacob after he had eaten of his venison.

'There is another important reason why I am writing

this letter to you. You must listen to me and do what I tell you. For you are my son. You must not take away your kinsman Simeon from Government work here in Ibala to another town. He is your kinsman and you must not do anything bad to him. Let him continue to do his work here at Ibala, that he may be near you. You must seek his advice in all things that you do for he knows Government work very well. He knows the world more than you do. Whenever he tells you not to do a thing you must not do it. And when he tells you to do a thing you should do it. I hear all the things you are doing to him and my mind is not pleased about it. I hear that you do not give him much respect. This is not good. When your father Samuel was alive and had not gone to answer the Saviour's call, Simeon gave him much respect. If your father Samuel told Simeon not to do anything he would not do it. So you too must respect him and do whatever he tells you to do. You must not take him away from Government work at Ibala to another town. I am an old man, and you must listen to my warning. If you do not listen to my warning there will be a curse on you. So you must listen to my warning that there may be no curse on you.

'All at home here greet you. Your mother greets you. Your brothers and your sisters and your servants. They all greet you. And they greet all your servants who live with you. They all greet you, without any exception. My words are finished. I am your father

Joel Tobatele.'

*

At evening service the following Sunday the vicar announced that an important member of the Church was requesting the prayers of the congregation for a very important thing. He wanted the congregation to pray for him that a certain thing which he desired in his work should be granted him by God Almighty and that a certain disaster which threatened his work should be averted. The member enclosed the sum of £1 with the request for the prayer. The vicar invited any elder of the Church to lead the congregation. They were all at various stages of getting down on their knees when the sonorous voice of Sister Deborah cried out from one of the front benches.

'God the Father, God the Son, God the Holy Ghost.'

'Amen,' the congregation chorused.

'The God of Abraham, and of Isaac and of Jacob.'

'Amen.'

'The same yesterday, the same today, and the same for everlasting, world without end—'

'Amen, Amen!'

'You know the secrets of all our hearts. Before we open our mouths You have known the things that we want to say. We are like little children who do not know the things that they want. But You are the everlasting Father that knows all the wants of Your children before they even mention the wants to You. We bring to You today before Your throne of grace the humble request of one of Your children of this Church. We do not know which of us it is, but You, Father, with eyes bigger than the eyes of several thousand elephants know him. We do not know the nature of his problem but You who can see much deeper than the greatest wizard knows his problems. We pray You, Father, to grant him whatever his request is—'

'Amen, Amen.'

'Help him to overcome all his enemies, Father.'

'Amen, Amen.'

'Drive away evil men from him in his work, Father'.

'Amen, Amen.'

'If he is in Government work do not let the spade of Government hurt his foot. (Amen, Amen.) Let his master the white man love him more and more. (Amen, Amen.) At the very sight of him let everyone like him. Let them love him and not hate him. (Amen, Amen.) Let his masters so like him that they will always give him more and more money. Let them overlook his mistakes; let them always remember only his good work—'

'Amen, Amen.'

'Father, watch him and his household – his wives, his children. If there are any of his wives that have no children, Father, please provide them with children. Do not visit them with the curse of children born to die again and again.'

'Amen, Amen.'

'Father, we want You to bless all of us members of this Church. We are all Your children. Bless us and do not curse us as You cursed Cain. You know the innermost secrets of all our hearts. Father, please grant to all of us Your children our several requests that we may give You thanks and glory—'

'Amen, Amen.'

'And when the day comes when we shall say good-bye to this world of sin and woe may we find mercy with You and be acceptable into Your fold up above, when we shall join the heavenly Choir singing, Glory, Glory, Lord God of Hosts. We ask it all in the name of Your only Son, Jesus Christ.'

'Amen, Amen, Amen.'

As they were all scrambling to their feet Pastor Morakinyo announced the next hymn. He read out the words line by line.

1. Through the love of God our Saviour,
   All will be well;

Free and changeless in His favour;
      All, all is well:
Precious is the blood that healed us;
Perfect is the grace that sealed us;
Strong the hand stretched forth to shield us;
      All must be well.

2. Though we pass through tribulation,
      All will be well;
Christ hath purchased full salvation,
      All, all is well:
Happy still in God confiding;
Fruitful, if in Christ abiding;
Holy, through the Spirit's guiding;
      All must be well.

Thirteen

———————◇———————

PROSSER, the District Officer, rang Titus and to his surprise spoke about Simeon's transfer. 'I hear that your foreman is going away,' he said. 'I shall not be sorry to see him go, I'll tell you. The man is a perfect rogue, and everyone in the station knows it. And what's more, he's damned incompetent. I think it's the best thing you've done. Transfer him away from here.'

'But I did not arrange the transfer. And to tell you the truth, Mr Prosser, I don't know where you get your information from.' He did not like Prosser. He knew he was a great gossip and he suspected that he was in the habit of giving adverse information about him and his work at Ibala to McBain at Ibadan.

'I must have heard from Ibadan, I imagine, even though when I was with McBain the other day I don't think he mentioned that to me. But never mind how I heard, Mr Oti. What matters is that the man is going. And no one here will be sorry to see the rogue go.'

'Oh yes.'

'And when he's gone, Mr Oti, you'll have a chance of reorganizing road maintenance – and I tell you it needs reorganizing. The Administration is just pouring scarce money down the drain, paying all those labourers that

that Foreman of yours keeps entering in his book. When I drove from Iwana to Ibala today I counted exactly three labourers. Three, d'ye hear? And only one of those three was working. The other two were sleeping under a tree.'

'Yes, Mr Prosser,' he commented, full of hate for the man. He was doing his best not to explode. According to protocol the District Officer was the most senior officer in the station. He was the local representative of His Majesty. In this capacity he interfered with everyone else's work.

'And the Resident has instructed me to speak to you about the state of funds generally. I've told both the Medical Officer and the Agricultural Officer what I'm now telling you. The Resident has directed that all officers must exert themselves and try to effect substantial savings on all votes. It is nearly certain now that there will be no augmentation to any votes this financial year. It is still highly confidential, but as a head of department I can let you have this secret: the Legislative Council will not pass the supplementary budget.'

'Really?'

'That's quite true. They will not pass the supplementary budget. Nothing to do with us, in a sense. It's that chap, the Second Member for Oyo Division in the House. It's he who makes such wild allegations about squandermania in Government departments.'

*

Meanwhile, the headmen of the various gangs organized the raising of funds among the labourers for financing what their secretary described as a rousing send-off for the foreman. Each headman was to pay 5s, and each labourer 3s. The money was to be deducted from source.

Through a standing agreement with the Union, collections were made this way, the labourer being paid his wages less the 3s or 5s whatever the levy for the month was.

The men of Gang Three on the Ibala–Ibadan Road debated the topical issue of Simeon's transfer. Three of them sat on the trunk of an *odan* tree that had been felled on the road verge. A fourth man lay on his back on the verge under the shade of a mango tree staring into the sky through the gaps in the foliage.

'So *Oga* Foreman is going after all – wonderful!' one of the three men on the tree trunk observed as he removed the stump of a cigar from his ear. He got up and moved to the remains of a fire over which they had roasted corn earlier in the day. He lit his cigar from one of the smouldering embers. He let out two puffs of smoke and felt elated. He walked back to his companions on the trunk. Then he concluded his observation: 'This Government has a lot of power.'

'Government work is not a good thing,' the man staring into the sky said, still lying flat on his back and still staring into the sky. '*Oga* Foreman has wives and children and he has a big farm. He is now to leave them and to go to another place. There's too much *wahala* in Government work.'

One of the other two men on the tree trunk grinned toothlessly at what those around him were saying. He always grinned at the things others around him said and did. He himself said little and did less. He was a relative of the Chief Clerk – by marriage.

'Government work – no use,' the man with the cigar muttered again. He spat on the floor, wiping some saliva off his cheek with the back of his left hand. 'No use at all. They transfer him not to Lagos, not to Ibadan, but to the bush in the Cameroons. I wouldn't take it if I were in his position. Thank God there are other things besides Government work.'

'That's how you talk all the time,' the third man on the tree trunk said contemptuously. 'Government work no use – Government work no use. If Government work is no use, why don't you leave it?'

The others laughed. The grinning man grinned. The man with the cigar was offended. 'Jacob, you come again,' he said. 'Have I said anything against you? I know you are *Oga* Foreman's brother. That's why you are ready to quarrel now.'

'You think far too much of your importance. Why don't you leave Government work and go back to your village?'

Again the others laughed. And again the grinning man grinned.

'I don't blame you, Jacob. You are a beast of no abode. It's my fault mixing up with poor people like you. When I become the *Oba* of my town in July next year you will see. The kingmakers have invited me to be the next *Oba*.'

'*Oba* of your town – ha, ha, ha—'

'But you told us the other day that you're going to England to study law,' one of the others observed. 'You are not going to England any more?'

'That's what he says. He will be *oba* of his town. He will go to England. He will do everything.'

'I want all of you to warn Jacob to desist from provoking me,' the lawyer-cum-*Oba*-elect said, extinguishing the smouldering end of his cigar. 'He's asking for trouble – and I'll give him plenty of it.'

'What trouble can you give me? Today you're going to England. Tomorrow—'

'You think I was joking when I said I was going to England? You don't know that I am taking a correspondence course with Wolsey Hall. In January I am sitting the London Matriculation Exam. And after that I go to Lincoln's Inn to study law. You think I'm a dunce like you, without any ambition? You wait till I come back from England as a qualified barrister; then you will see.' He had been gesticulating all along with the cigar. Now he placed it behind his left ear.

'Why will you two kill yourselves, anyway?' the man still lying down said. '*Oga* Foreman who's going on transfer has not taken it as seriously as you are now taking it.' The man did not get up, nor stop staring into the sky as he aired his views.

'*Bo* "lawyer", I want you to lend me 5s,' Jacob said. They all laughed. But Jacob protested that he was not joking at all. He needed 10s, and needed it very badly. He said that his wife had been to hospital for three days running without seeing the doctor. A nurse had told her that she was wasting her time as there were far too many people waiting to see the overworked doctor and that the doctor had no real medicines in the hospital. If she cared to come to his house as a private patient the nurse would give her a course of injections and she would be well again. All this for 10s.

They heard his story. They sympathized with him but they were not surprised to hear it. For congestion at the few ill-equipped hospitals, and the habit of nurses and dispensers and ward servants parading themselves as doctors was known to every one of them.

Then Jacob appealed to the grinning man. They were all interested in the reaction of the grinning man. For they knew that money-lending was his real business; his employment as a road labourer was only a camouflage. Yes, he was ready to loan Jacob the 10s on the usual terms, which were that starting with the following pay day and on every subsequent pay day Jacob was to pay an interest of 2s 6d on the 10s. This would continue every month till Jacob was in a position to make a final single payment of 12s 6d representing that month's interest of 2s 6d and the capital of 10s. They were all witnesses to the transaction, as they watched the grinning man bring out a dirty wallet from the pocket of his trousers and from it he counted out ten coins to Jacob.

Jacob retired into the bush so that his companions should not see into which of his pockets he disposed of the money. As he returned to his place one of his colleagues was observing loudly that Jacob was not going to pay the money back. Jacob was about to start another quarrel when the man explained why he said so. 'You see, the Day of Judgement is coming next month. You remember Bandele's vision. He saw the Coming of Judgement Day.'

'That was foolish talk,' the law student commented. 'And only foolish, illiterate people believe in such foolish talk.'

'But *Oga* Foreman was there. And what's more, D.E. himself was there. Everybody now knows that the world is coming to an end.'

The grinning man again distributed a grin behind which it was difficult to discern whether he was alarmed or indifferent to the impending doom. The man who lay on his back challenged the authenticity of the story of Judgement Day coming as soon as the following month. He said that he had met Bandele since his vision and had confirmed that it was to be four months and seventeen days from the date of the vision, and not one month.

After a short silence the lawyer-to-be again declared that it was only illiterate people who believed in such nonsense.

'If even the world comes to an end next month we

would have held the send-off function for *Oga* Foreman. So we still have to pay.'

'You see, all they will give us at the function is palm wine. *Oga* Foreman and the headmen will drink all the gin and the whisky.'

'And what's wrong with that?' the man staring into the sky asked. 'It is Allah that put *Oga* Foreman in a big position. It is Allah that put all the headmen in big positions. And it is Allah that put D.E. above them all,' he concluded philosophically.

'But look at that small boy, the District Engineer. This world is a funny place.'

'He earns over £1,000 every month.'

'One thousand pounds! What does he do with £1,000 every month? He has no wife, no children. He puts all his money in the bank.'

Jacob said, 'He has taken that lady contractor, the one they call Auntie Bimp, from *Oga* Foreman. He gives to her most of his money.'

'Wait, listen,' one of them warned.

They all stopped suddenly. They strained their ears. There was no mistaking it, for they heard the whistle a second time. Its blast rent the air, from somewhere high up in the mango tree. And far, far away they saw the car approaching.

They scrambled to their feet and made for their spades and their headpans. By the time the approaching car drove into their midst the men of Gang Three were working hard.

It was the District Engineer. He stopped to see what they were doing. 'Where's your headman?' he asked.

'Gone to hospital, sir.'

'There are five men in your gang. Where's the fifth man?' he asked Jacob.

'He has gone to the latrine, sir.'

Although Titus suspected that the fifth man had certainly not gone to the latrine as there were no latrines in the bush, he did not suspect that this man was keeping sentinel watch up in the mango tree to warn his comrades of the approach of anyone in authority.

Fourteen

———————◇———————

Titus was unhappy about the Simeon transfer business in particular, and about Simeon in general. He hated Simeon because of his corruption and the ineffectiveness of his supervision of his subordinates. It was his corruption and his inefficiency that gave the District Officer the chance to speak to Titus the way he did and the chance of interfering with his work generally.

It would be a relief if the Foreman were transferred. But as he had explained – to many people – he was not personally responsible for the transfer, despite the rumours which had filled both Ibadan and Ibala. Moreover he was nearly certain there was no substance in it whatsoever.

Thomas his steward-cook handed him a letter as he sank into a chair one afternoon when he arrived home from his work. He tore open the envelope and pulled out the two sheets of writing paper. He frowned as he read the first few lines. Apparently this was not a love letter; it was not an application for a job or for registration as a contractor. He swore as he got up and picked up his helmet; without touching his lunch, he left the house and jumped into his car, leaving Thomas disgruntled and muttering on the verandah.

He drove straight to the vicarage. Cutting short the exchange of any pleasantries with the vicar he went immediately to the point, 'I know you are surprised to see me here today, sir. I'm sorry about it all. I'm much too busy. That's why I don't come here very often.'

'I see. And, I understand. But, my dear Titus, come to church sometimes. I'm sure you can manage once a month.'

After a little hesitation Titus said, 'I shall try.'

'And you told me that you will come to advise about the church building from time to time, Engineer. You've been too busy, I know. Brother Simeon tells me how busy you've been.'

'My Foreman Simeon!' he nearly cried. 'It is on account of him that I've come, Vicar. I must talk to you frankly.'

'Oh yes,' the vicar said in apprehension. 'It isn't true you are transferring him, Engineer?'

'That's the story everywhere! I'm transferring Simeon my Foreman. I'm transferring Simeon my Foreman. It was bad enough people saying it as individuals. But why should the Church as a body complicate this already complicated and sordid affair? Speaking frankly I'm disappointed, sir. I'm disappointed.'

'The Church? I do not understand,' the vicar said, sincerely perplexed.

'Then read this, sir,' he thrust the letter into the vicar's hand. 'Read that, sir.'

This was what the old man read:

'To Titus Oti, our dear Brother in Christ.

'We are the members of All Souls Church, Ibala, and we write this letter to you that you may read the letter and turn back from your bad ways and turn to God by following the way of salvation.

'Your father Samuel Oti was a good man and a

leader in this Church. And when he died the whole church accorded him a well-befitting funeral. We know that because of his good deeds here on earth, he is now sitting on the right hand of God the Father Almighty, singing Holy, Holy, Holy, in the heavenly choir.

'When you came back from the white man's country with education and qualifications as great as those of the white man, we as a church welcomed you back. We all joined in the thanksgiving to God for bringing you back safe, and for all the glory you brought to our town and to our church.

'We explained to you our problems and our hope that you would help us solve them. We wanted you to help with our church building. We wanted you to show a good example for all the other educated youths to follow. Instead of doing this you have shamelessly ignored this church. We want you to pray to God that He and His church may not ignore you.

'We have watched the very uncharitable way in which you have been behaving to Brother Simeon Oke who is one of the strongest pillars of this church. You have ignored the fact that he was the brother of your late father. You have done many things to shame him in his work in your office.

'Now because you want to take his woman from him you have planned to transfer him from Ibala to a very distant place called the Cameroons. Because of the love you have for his woman you want to commit this crime to him and to the Church. Yet you know that if he goes away we shall suffer very much in the work of the building of the House of the Lord.

'We want you to read Second Samuel, Chapter Eleven and Chapter Twelve. Because David coveted Bathsheba the daughter of Eliam and wife of Uriah the Hittite, David commanded Joab to put Uriah in the hottest part of the battle that he might be slain. And Uriah was slain and David took unto himself Bathsheba the wife of Uriah.

'And because of David's sin against Uriah the Hittite·the Lord cursed David, saying that the sword would never depart from his house and that He would raise up evil against him out of his own house.

'Titus Oti, son of Elder Samuel, we warn you to desist from your evil ways. We warn you to leave alone Brother Simeon Oke and his woman. We warn you to stop your evil intention to transfer him from his wives and children here in Ibala to a foreign place called the Cameroons where there is no food and people eat only plantains and bananas.

'Repent, Brother Titus, for there is forgiveness for the sinner that repenteth.'

'Now that you have read it, sir, you understand what I've been saying. This really must stop. It is getting out of hand. It must *stop*.' Titus showed his annoyance.

'Engineer,' the vicar said. 'Engineer, you must listen to me.'

But the man found great difficulty in saying whatever it was he wanted the young man to listen to. He continued eventually, 'Engineer, I am very sorry about this letter.'

'Then you know all about it, sir. This, sir . . .'

'Oh no, my dear Engineer. Not at all,' the vicar protested.

'But you are sorry about it. The church is sorry about it. This, I imagine, is all I'm going to get from the church. My name has been dragged in the mud. This amounts to defamation of character, sir. And what do I get for it? That's what I want to know from you, sir!'

'But, Engineer, you are not dragging the church to court? You are a member of the church – Ah, Elder Abraham, welcome to you. And you, Elder Joel.'

Titus noticed that his great-uncle carried his walking-stick and that the other man carried an umbrella as they came in. The other man said: 'Reverend, we were going to see Elder Matthew. He has been ill for some time. We saw you and Engineer talking. So we said we would stop to pay our respects to you, Reverend.'

'I thank you both, Elders. You are welcome.'

Pa Joel sank into a chair.

'I hope it is not a serious matter you are discussing, Reverend, that Engineer here sees his aged father without remembering to say his greetings to him?'

Titus said, 'Greetings to you, this evening, Pa.'

Pa Joel hissed back. 'It is not me that you have shamed but Deborah, your mother. Even though I am an old man without any money I must have the proper respects due to me. If your father Samuel saw me anywhere he would break away from whatever he was doing, run to me, and prostrate in greetings.'

Rev. Morakinyo said: 'Pa Joel, we were discussing a very important matter. Please don't be annoyed about Engineer not greeting you properly.'

Elder Abraham supported the vicar. 'You must not think seriously of this matter. He is an *alakowe*. If you greet them they seldom answer. This is the reason why they live in the place where white men live. There they live all alone. They hear no one. They speak to no one.'

'But, Abraham, I want you to be fair in this matter,' Pa Joel said. 'When you say that he is an *alakowe*, is he a greater *alakowe* than Reverend here?'

'No,' Abraham admitted.

'If a railway train runs for a hundred years without stopping, will it not find that land is always still ahead of it? Can the learning of Titus ever reach that of Reverend, no matter how many books he may read, and in spite of the number of times he may go to the country of the white man? And does Reverend not still say greetings to us when he sees us? That is why you must judge the case properly.'

Rev. Morakinyo noticed that Titus was becoming impatient. He said: 'Fathers, I want you to know that Engineer has been made very angry over a certain matter. And that was what we were discussing when you came. Someone has written a letter to accuse him of trying to transfer Brother Simeon Oke. And they also say that he is doing this because there is a woman in the case. It is a very important thing, Fathers, as Engineer Titus is very much distressed over it.'

All four were silent for some time. A little girl came from the kitchen area of the vicarage and ran to the vicar saying 'Papa, papa.'

'What is most important is that this letter has been written by someone who says he is the Secretary of the Church,' Rev. Morakinyo said. 'And, and – run away to your mother now— And this appears to Mr Titus Oti as meaning that I and all the church are behind the letter. I would like to say here before all of you that I knew nothing about this letter.'

They were again all silent for a moment. Pa Joel was uneasy in his chair. He had not completely recovered from the shame of the lack of respect that his erring young relative had shown him. Then Elder Abraham said: 'Reverend, I am an old man, I want you to heed my words. You must not allow woman trouble to wreck our church. We must settle the matter well between the two brothers. My words are finished, Reverend.'

Pa Joel supported his age-group. 'Women. Terrible creatures,' he hissed. 'When I first heard of this matter, I called Deborah. I warned her to go and speak to this boy that he may escape the clutches of that bad woman from Ibadan. Is it a good thing for two brothers to run after the same woman? Reverend, is it a good thing? That woman is going to ruin my household. That was why I told Deborah to go and tell her son to leave the woman alone. She belongs to Simeon. And Simeon is his kinsman. You see my trouble?'

Titus now became very angry indeed. He addressed the vicar in English. 'When I came to you I did so in the hope that you would do something about this most vexatious and libellous document that has been addressed to me by someone in your church. Instead you have brought in these old men to confuse the issue. I tell you I shall not take this lying down. I am certainly going to see a lawyer about it—'

'Oh, my dear Titus!'

'And I tell you one thing about this man Simeon Oke whom you and your church think is next to Jesus Christ in character. The man that is so wonderful, that must not be transferred. He is a most incompetent person. Worse than that, he is a rogue. When he steals money from Government he brings half of it to your church. He pockets the remaining half—'

'Enough, enough,' Pa Joel cried from his chair. Both he and Elder Abraham had been looking at the mouth of Titus while the words flowed. They did not understand what he said. But they understood enough to know that they were angry words against Simeon, against the vicar, against the church. 'I shall not sit here while the son of Samuel uses the white man's language to abuse our Reverend and all of us. Whatever is the world coming to?' he asked, panting fury. 'If a dog runs mad, does he not recognize and run away from fire? Even if you've been to Jerusalem the heavenly city, beyond the White man's Country, do you not know that your learning is nothing compared with that of our Reverend? And you dare stand up in argument with our Reverend – you – you—'

'Father, please, father,' Rev. Morakinyo cried and sprang to his feet to intercept the blow that the old man had aimed at his grandnephew. But, by this time Titus had stormed out of the vicarage and driven away in his car in great anger.

Fifteen

———————◇———————

THE Rev. Michael Morakinyo prayed for heavenly guidance in the crisis that was rapidly engulfing his church. The new church building of All Souls had been the one consuming passion of his pastoral career. He had dreamt of it ever since he was training as a sub-pastor. He had planned for it ever since he had been working as a junior member of the clergy in one of the smaller churches in the Diocese. And since he was pro-moted to be vicar of All Souls, the mother church of the Diocese, he had brought his great organizing ability, his oratory in the pulpit, and his charm and personality to bear on the one problem, all working towards the same objective – of building a new All Souls Church worthy of its name and worthy of its position.

'The Church's one foundation is Jesus Christ her Lord' was the processional hymn sung at the ceremony of the laying of the foundation stone of the new building. Michael Morakinyo had led his congregation at the singing of that hymn in the presence of a large number of his brother clergy and the Diocesan Bishop. He had always known that after the foundation had been laid every bit of the material superstructure had borne the stamp of Simeon Oke – every bit of the edifice as it grew. He belonged to the Church Building Committee. And as a member of that committee he had been responsible for most of the ideas that had brought in large sums of money.

Unfortunately he had also been responsible for the idea that had brought in Titus Oti as a member of the committee. But not only had the young engineer failed to give large sums of money to the building fund, it would now appear that he might in fact be actively working against the interests of the church. How else could anyone interpret the rumour that Simeon Oke was to be transferred to the Cameroons? There, in that very distant place, he would be most ineffective as far as the Church building was concerned.

The vicar realized that a most delicate situation had arisen which required both tact and heavenly guidance. If only others had left him to handle the matter himself he was certain he would have succeeded in winning Titus to his side. He sighed at such a chain of misfortunes. If someone had not written the letter which had put Titus's back up; if only Pa Joel and Elder Abraham had not come into his study the very moment he was discussing the matter with Titus, he was sure things could have been settled amicably. He would also have put in a word or two for Simeon and tried to influence Titus to see that the transfer did not take effect.

The trouble was, the reverend gentleman thought, that both Pa Joel and Sister Deborah had persisted in making the mistake of always regarding Titus as their little boy and not as the important Titus Oti, Esq., B.Sc. (Eng.), District Engineer of Ibala P.W.D. He himself at first had made the mistake of still thinking of Titus Oti as the little choir-boy that he had once caned for not singing properly at choir practice. But after a few weeks he had known better.

Apart from the trouble over Simeon Oke's transfer there was the Bandele vision and the unrest it had stirred up among the congregation of All Souls. The *Alasotele* movement in Elder Matthew's house had started as an innocent prayer meeting. Elder Matthew had specialized in leading the Church Congregation in the extempore prayers in which someone or the other was always asking the prayer of the church for God's mercy on his work or God's guidance in a new project or thankfulness for recovery from an illness. All this used to happen only on Sundays, once at morning service and once at evening service. But soon Elder Matthew began midweek prayer meetings at his own house.

There was nothing wrong with all this, in a sense, and Pastor Morakinyo did not feel at all worried. Not, at least, until he began to hear strange tales of people seeing visions at Elder Matthew's prayer meetings; visions such as dead relatives who sent messages back to their living relations to observe certain rites that bore close affinity to customs which the Rev. Morakinyo could only describe as pagan.

The latest of these was the Bandele vision. Again there was nothing seriously wrong in a devout Christian seeing a vision of the Day of Judgement. But half the Congregation of All Souls had now come to take Bandele's vision to mean that the end of the world was imminent and that it was only a matter of a few weeks or a few months. Some people were already planning how the Last Day might find them engaged in religious exercises that would score them good marks and make them acceptable to God. Pastor Morakinyo's fear was that these people could not sustain their religious enthusiasm indefinitely and would, in disappointment, fall well below their normal, and acceptable, pitch of religious observance.

This was the background to the silent prayer of the Vicar of All Souls before he set out for the special meeting of the church. This, too, was the background against which he read out to the meeting the words of the first verse of the hymn that opened the proceedings:

> 'Lead us, heavenly Father, lead us,
> O'er the world's tempestuous sea;
> Guard us, guide us, keep us, feed us,
> For we have no help but Thee;
> Yet possessing every blessing,
> If our God our Father be.'

After the hymn, he invoked God the Father, God the Son and God the Holy Ghost to come down and intervene in the very serious matter of the tragedy that threatened the Church of All Souls. He recalled how He, the God of Abraham and of Isaac and of Jacob, had stood by Elijah and had not delivered him into the hands of the wicked woman Jezebel. He recalled how He had stood by Shadrach, Meshach and Abednego in the strange land of Babylon – how He, the Great Lord, had delivered Daniel from the lions' den, how He had delivered Jonah from the fish's stomach after He had subjected him to the terrors of the waves for three days and three nights. He recalled how He, the great Lord, had subjected Job to serious trials and tribulations but had at the end brought him out triumphant and untarnished. Had God Almighty not subjected His only Son to the great trial by the Devil for forty days and forty nights in the wilderness? And did He the great Father not bring out Christ triumphant at the end of it?

His Church on earth was passing through difficult times. That section of his Church located in Ibala was, indeed, passing through a crisis. It was not the first time that had happened to the Church of Christ. He recalled the persecution of the early Christians immediately after the Ascension. He recalled the terrible atrocities committed against the Early Church by Emperor Nero of Rome. But had the Lord God not seen to it that the Church rode triumphant over these waves of persecution? He called on the Lord God of Jacob to come down at that moment and foil the machinations of the Evil One who was responsible for the unhappy state of affairs in the Church. He said many other things, all of them punctuated by *Amens* from the elders assembled in the church vestry.

Simeon himself had an entirely different line of approach to his problem. He had no doubt that his kinsman the District Engineer was at the bottom of his troubles. He had grave doubts, however, about the efficacy of the prayers and deliberations of Pastor Morakinyo and the elders of the church when a person of the heartlessness of young Titus Oti was involved. He decided to fight his battle from the P.W.D. Headquarters at Ibadan, from where flowed the stream of authority to Ibala and the other districts.

He was quite tired by the time he entered the outskirts of Ibadan in his old Prefect. He had strained his eyes trying to avoid lorries that refused to dip their lights. Now on the outskirts he dodged sheep and goats that lay in groups on the carriageway completely unmindful of the death-dealing propensities of his car. He drove on along the Taffy Jones highway for some distance before turning into a back street. He parked the car under a big *odan* tree, wound up the windows and climbed out of the driver's seat. He pulled out a walking-stick from under the back seat. He proceeded to tap his way along another furlong of very bad road. It was a moonlight night and little children were still playing hide-and-seek on the verandahs of houses and in the shadows of a group of mango trees.

He entered the yard leading to the outhouses of a big two-storey building. He noticed that a number of people were lying on mats on the concrete verandah. Outside the door of the second of the six rooms a woman sat down, knitting. He made for her and asked for Mr Odiachi.

'Mr Odiachi?' the woman looked puzzled. 'Where does he work?'

'P.W.D.'

'P.W.D.; you mean Samson?'

Simeon did not know Odiachi's Christian name. He took a chance and said yes. The woman then told him to knock at the fifth door.

After he had knocked at the fifth door for the third time a female voice said from within: 'He is not in. Who should I say has called?'

'His friend from Ibala,' Simeon said.

There was some movement in the room, followed by the rustling of clothes and the striking of a match. Eventually the door was opened only sufficiently to allow a head to peep out. The owner of the head held a lantern up and said: 'Good evening, who do you want?' He was suspicious of the caller.

Simeon moved nearer as he said, 'You do not remember me, sir? I am the Foreman from Ibala.'

'Ah, it's you, my friend,' the man Samson said in recognition. He opened the door a little wider. 'I did not know it was you, sir. One must be careful these days, you know. Come in, come in, sir, my missis and I are happy to see you in our house. Come in, sir.'

The room, the bye-law minimum size of twelve by ten, was partitioned into two with a curtain, the timber bed occupying one half while three chairs and a table occupied the other. Boxes and cooking utensils competed for space under the bed and at its foot.

The woman clambered out of bed carrying a wailing child who could not understand this disturbance of its slumbers.

'I thank you for remembering to come to see me today, sir,' Samson Odiachi said, as he sat at the edge of the bed. 'It is kind of you, sir.'

'You know I promised the other day to see you often,' Simeon said getting up from his chair and sitting next to Odiachi on the bed. 'We must remember the people in the office who are good to us,' he said edging his way nearer Odiachi. 'You see,' he said as he brought out an envelope from his trousers' pocket, 'a child that shows gratitude for yesterday's favour will receive yet another today.' He placed the envelope on the table. 'We are in the field and in the bush. We see nothing, we know nothing. You in the office see everything and know everything. You in the office are our eyes. We must see with your eyes. And we must show our gratitude.'

'Oh, thank you, sir, thank you, sir,' Odiachi said happily. 'What shall I offer you to drink now?'

'Let's leave drinks first,' Simeon suggested. 'Let us discuss a very important matter which you must help me about.' He moved nearer still to his host as he related his story. They both discussed the matter in whispers.

Later that night both Simeon and Odiachi called to see Isaac George the Chief Clerk. Samson apologized to the Chief that they had come so late at night. But the matter was very pressing. 'So I thought he should see you himself.'

'It is about the transfer, *Oga*,' Simeon said, rising up from his chair and prostrating before the Chief. 'It is about the transfer that I have come. At a time like this one must look for a man that is competent to save one. And that is why I have sought you tonight. You are my master and my father.'

'Get up, get up,' the Chief told him.

When he got up Simeon noticed that Odiachi had left the room. 'I want you, *Oga*, to save me from the evil machinations of Titus Oti,' he said fumbling for something in his pocket. He brought out another envelope, bulkier than the one he had left at Samson's. He put it on a drinks stool as he said: 'Please do not transfer me from Ibala.'

The Chief looked away from the envelope on the stool. He rose and walked to the window. He opened it slightly and peeped out. Some children were playing on the verandah below. It appeared to him that no one was about. He closed the window and came back to his seat. He adjusted his coverlet round his left shoulder. 'But why have you behaved like a small boy, Mr Oke? Why are you bringing the matter to me now that it is nearly too late?'

'I beg you, *Oga*. Forgive me. I am late, but nothing is too late for you to handle.'

'It is a difficult matter. A very difficult matter, I tell you.'

'I know. But there's nothing too difficult for *Oga Agba* to do in the P.W.D. And I promise I shall come to show my gratitude.'

'It is difficult, very difficult,' the Chief Clerk said, nodding his head as a measure of the difficulty of stopping Simeon's transfer. 'But I'll see what I can do for you, Mr Oke.'

Simeon returned to Ibala in the early hours of the morning. He was very tired. But he could not afford to sleep much in the little that remained of the night. Before cock-crow he was consulting old Sunmonu, the

most famous professional diviner and *juju*-man in Ibala
and district. Sunmonu was used to clients calling at that
unholy hour of the night. He was also used to church-
going members of the community coming to consult
him at night over problems of employment or barrenness
in women or witchcraft. He listened to Simeon's story
and his request that he should use his powers to stop
the transfer.

Sunmonu asked a few questions about the relations
between him and his kinsman Titus Oti. He told Simeon
that the easiest solution to the problem was to make the
juju get Titus Oti himself transferred to the Cameroons
and he Simeon would then become District Engineer.
'Nobody likes him here in Ibala. He is much too strict.
People do not speak well of him.'

Simeon was ambitious, but he knew enough of Public
Works practice to know that Government would not
approve of a Road Foreman changing places with an
Engineer. The *juju* might be asked to undertake the impossible and then fail. He told Sunmonu that all he
wanted of him was to arrange that he was not transferred. He knew his men liked him, and the towns-
people liked him. He wanted Sunmonu to make this
popularity grow and spread from the workers to the
P.W.D. authorities themselves. If Sunmonu could arrange
that everyone from the Director and the Provincial
Engineer down to the lowliest artisan in the P.W.D.,
and everyone living and working in Ibala from the *Oba*
and his chiefs down to the smallest child should love and
talk well of him, then he was sure that the transfer would
be averted. Sunmonu indicated that he would accept
the assignment.

'Is it not our wont to dance for joy, whenever we see
a new-born babe?' he prefaced his incantations with the
first of a series of questions in poetic *Yoruba*:

'Has the eternal Creator not completed
His great work of creating us
before the Destroyer appeared on the scene?
And when the Destroyer appeared on the scene,
Were we not already safe in the
Strong arms of the Mender and the Repairer?
Can the diviner–priest ever lose his temper so furiously
That he will throw away his divining paraphernalia?
Is there any medicine man that would throw away his stock
    of medicines,
In a fit of anger no matter how severe?
Is it not with excitement that a child rejoices
On being given a bird to pet?
Does a child ever look with disdain upon a flamboyant
    flower?
Is it not true that the monkey leaps forward ever, and
    backward never?
Is it not true that the ram charges forward ever, and
    backward never?
Is it not true that whatever project the chameleon under-
    takes
Is blessed by the gods?'

Old Sunmonu told Simeon his fees – seven pounds, seven shillings and seven pennies all to be in white coins; two white rams without any black spots, four white cocks; two bottles of whisky and one of gin.

The following night Simeon went to bed with an easy mind for the first time for many days, certain that the combined effect of the prayers of Rev. Morakinyo and his church, the manipulations by the Chief Clerk of the papers in the Provincial Engineer's Office and old Sunmonu's *juju* would certainly do the trick.

But two days after he was arrested by the Police.

Sixteen

———————◇———————

IT was Pastor Morakinyo who took the news of Simeon's arrest to Titus. He jumped off his bicycle in the drive of Titus's bungalow and without waiting to park it properly ran up the four steps leading to the sitting-room and fairly battered at the door. When it was opened by Thomas, he cried. 'The Engineer. I want the Engineer.'

'Sit down, sir,' Thomas told him. 'I shall call master.'

'Tell Engineer to come quickly. Very important.'

Titus was in the bedroom, trying on a new pair of trousers that his tailor had sent him from Ibadan. He recognized the voice and the urgency in it.

'Brother Titus,' the clergyman said in anguish. 'They have arrested him. We must act quickly.'

'They have arrested him,' Titus repeated after him, not understanding. 'They have arrested whom?'

'Brother Simeon. They have arrested Brother Simeon.'

'Arrested Simeon?' Titus cried in astonishment. 'Who arrested him?'

'The Police. They have arrested him. Engineer, you must do something. Please save him.' Pastor Morakinyo was truly agitated.

'But, Pastor, why have they arrested him?'

He realized at once that this was a silly question.

While he himself knew a thousand and one reasons why the rogue should have been arrested and put behind bars long before now, Morakinyo did not know, or refused to know, that the Foreman was a rogue. He therefore could hardly expect him to admit any reason for the Police to arrest Simeon.

'Is he now at the police station?'

'Yes, in Ibadan. They—'

'They've taken him to Ibadan?'

'Yes, in a police van. Brother Titus, we've got to do something. They did not give me the chance to consult the church elders. Terrible, very terrible.'

Titus rang the Assistant Superintendent of Police in Ibala for information. The Superintendent confirmed that Simeon had been arrested, but he himself didn't have much information because it was a headquarters case and the local police knew very little about it. He knew Simeon had been taken to Ibadan and was in custody. He attempted ringing Ibadan but he was told by the telephone exchange that the trunk line to Ibadan was out of order. He banged the receiver in disgust.

A few minutes later he was motoring the thirty-seven miles between Ibadan and Ibala, with Pastor Morakinyo at his side. Neither said very much on the journey, but they both thought different thoughts about the same man. Titus was going to Ibadan more to please his companion than out of any conviction that Simeon was worth getting out of trouble. He thought that he was already compromising himself. Why should he not allow the law to take its course? He did not know for which of a multitude of crimes his kinsman had been arrested. He had known that sooner or later the law would catch up with him? Why, then, was he now worried that the inevitable had happened?

One aspect of the case made him angry. Why was it

that all this had happened to an officer under him without himself, the District Engineer, knowing about it before? He concluded that Prosser, the District Officer, must be at the bottom of this lack of confidence in his integrity. He was certain that if he had been white he would not have been treated in this way. The black man had not yet been accepted by Prosser and his clique of white officials as someone good enough to be trusted with secrets and confidences.

At the Iddo Gate police station the desk sergeant told Titus to write down details of his complaint on a form he gave him. But after a long time he accepted his explanation that he had not come to make any complaint, but that he had only come to make an inquiry about a P.W.D. man who was arrested at Ibala earlier that day. The sergeant told them that he heard about the case but he was not handling it and he directed the two men from Ibala to the office of his superior officer.

Pastor Morakinyo sighed in disappointment when, on being shown into the Superintendent's office, they discovered that he was an expatriate. He wore a military moustache which was neatly trimmed. His khaki was newly laundered, and the crown shone well on the sleeves.

'I understand you want to discuss bail for Mr Simeon Oke. I'm sorry about the whole thing, Mr Oti. But investigations are still proceeding. I must not allow bail at this stage. Procedure, you know,' he said, offering a cigarette to Titus. 'Police procedure, I'm afraid.'

'How soon can one bail him out then?' Titus asked, taking a cigarette.

'How soon? Oh, tomorrow afternoon, tomorrow evening – depends on how we get on.'

'Brother Simeon sleep in custody!' Pastor Morakinyo exclaimed. 'Engineer, you must persuade him to release Brother Simeon tonight. We must.'

'Absolutely impossible, Reverend. I'm sorry about it, but we must keep Mr Simeon Oke here tonight. And, Mr Oti, I do hope you know that under the Civil Service Code you are not competent to stand bail for another civil servant. You cannot therefore stand bail for your Foreman. But—'

'Can I not?'

'You cannot,' he said tapping the end of his cigarette lightly on the desk. 'But of course the vicar can. Men in holy orders, justices of the peace, and so on. But not civil servants.'

The following day Pastor Morakinyo bailed Simeon out.

Titus learnt the reason for Simeon's arrest from a letter from the Provincial Headquarters. Titus recognized the McBain initials over the stamp on the O.H.M.S. envelope. He tore it open and read the short letter inside.

'Attached please find copy of a letter from one Mr Jacob of Ibala and addressed to the Hon. Director of Public Works, with copies sent to the Resident and the Oba of Ibala. You will see that Mr Jacob has made serious allegations in this document. You are requested to investigate the allegations as a matter of urgency and to send your report to me in quadruplicate in accordance with Chapter Nine paragraphs 113–121 of Government Procedure. Meanwhile you are to confirm that you are observing the appropriate provisions of Stores Regulations and Supervision of Labour.'

Titus next read the attachment:

'Your Honour, I am your Honour's very obedient and very humble servant. I am not fit to write a letter to your Honour because I am a lowly employee in your Honour's very big Department and Empire. So pardon me, your Honour.

'But if someone should ask: what has made little Mr Jacob take his pen to write a letter to the Director who is the biggest *oga* in the P.W.D. my answer is simple and short: honesty, patriotism and fairplay. Your Honour knows that honesty is the best policy. Also the love of fatherland, which is patriotism, is the greatest love – it even surpasses the love of women. And finally, your Honour, as you are a Britisher and the British are famous for their love of fair play, I appeal to the sense of fair play in you.

'In Ibala P.W.D. there is no honesty and there is no fair play. There is very serious dishonesty and man's inhumanity to man. The man that is responsible for the absence of these two elements is not Mr Titus Oti the District Engineer. Everyone here in Ibala knows that he is an honest man and a God-fearing man. The real troublemaker is none other than Mr Simeon Oke the Foreman. He is the one that does not know moderation in his dishonesty. He takes money from right and from left. And when he cannot please both right and left at the same time, trouble comes.

'On his cocoa farm near Iwana about seven miles from Ibala he is using P.W.D. labourers to work on the farm. Even I know the names of some of them. This is dishonesty your Honour.

'His car is no longer working. Yet he tells lies by saying that he uses the car to run many miles for Government work. He claims a lot of money from Government this way. The District Engineer, who does not know his trick, approves his mileage allowance. The Foreman is a perfect crook, your Honour.

'It is because I have the fire of patriotism burning in me that I write this letter to your Honour. I want you to employ the usual British sense of justice and fair-play to stop Mr Simeon Oke's dishonesty in Ibala. Your Honour should arrange to investigate what I have said in this letter and you will find them true. Can I, an honest man, write things that are not true? Impossible. So act quickly, in the interest of the many million inhabitants of this great country.'

Seventeen

———————◇———————

DEBORAH was ill.

News of his mother's illness reached Titus in a note from Pastor Morakinyo and he hurried down to see her.

She was alone in the room. Titus had been worried for some time about the fact that very few people now lived in the family house. His mother might die of a sudden illness before anyone raised the alarm.

He stood at the door of her room for a while to get used to the poor illumination, which came from a clay lamp placed on an inverted bowl at the far end of the room.

She lay on her left side on a mat on the floor, with one of her old cover-cloths rolled into a pillow. He noticed that she wore no blouse and that her loin-cloth covered her only from the waist down.

'Mother, you must cover your chest. I've always told you it's dangerous not to.'

She did not answer. She appeared neither surprised nor interested in his appearance. He went in, and sat near her. It was a difficult process for someone used to sitting on chairs and stools to sit on a mat on a hard floor, leaning his back against the black-painted wall and stretching his legs along the floor. He remembered that he used to find sitting up and sleeping in that room not so difficult – when he was a schoolboy at Ibala. That was many years before.

'Mother, what's wrong with you?' he asked.

'I'm well. There's nothing wrong with me.' She still did not look up at him.

'But Pastor sent a note round to me to say you are ill. What's the matter?'

She did not answer. He lit a cigarette.

'Mother, I want you to come with me to the hospital now. The doctor will examine you, and give you medicine.'

'I do not want you to worry me, Titus. When Pastor came here in the morning and mentioned my going to the hospital, I told him the truth about the matter. Now you too want me to go to the hospital. It's no use.'

'What's no use, Mother?'

'Going to the hospital. It's no use.'

'Why is it no use?'

'Titus, I know what's wrong with me,' she stirred. She next changed with difficulty from one side to the other. 'The disease that I'm suffering from is one for which the doctor in the hospital has no medicine. I know it.'

'But, Mother, I wish you wouldn't talk like a little girl – or like a doting old woman,' he said angrily, his usual impatience with his mother mounting. 'If you, my Mother, will not go to hospital when you are ill, then you may well die not of a disease but of your folly and stubbornness.'

'Now I want to ask you something,' she said, dragging herself to a sitting posture. 'Does a mouse follow one to one's room to bite one? Why do you follow me to my own room to insult me? Is this not the room allocated to me in the house built by my husband before he died?

Is this the house given to you by the white man who gave you the important work which you do and which has now gone into your head?'

'Mother, you must try and understand me,' he said as patiently as he could. 'You are ill. And if anyone is ill only the doctor can tell what's wrong with him, and what will cure him. Therefore, let me take you now to the doctor, and he will cure you.'

She burst into tears. He was surprised and worried. 'Why are you crying, Mother?' he asked.

'When I come to your house you call me foolish. Now you come to my husband's house and you call me a little girl and a doting old woman,' she sobbed. 'I am foolish. Pastor is foolish – you know more than he does. Your father's father is foolish. Simeon Oke has been in Government work before you went to school. He too is foolish. Everyone is foolish.'

'Mother, stop this nonsense. And get ready for the hospital,' he said, quite exhausted.

'There's something I must tell you, Titus, before you tell your P.W.D. workers to force me into your car and take me to the hospital. Simeon Oke who you are taking to court and who you—'

'Stop it, Mother, I am not taking anyone to court. It's the Police; it has nothing to do with me.'

'Who sent the Police? Is it not you who sent the Police after him? Tell me that.'

'Oh God, you too join them, Mother. Terrible!'

'And have I not heard that you are going to court to give evidence against him, that he may be sent to prison? You must listen to me. I will tell you today what I have not told you before,' she said. She adjusted herself painfully. He looked at her and had a feeling that she was possessed of some supernatural power.

'Simeon Oke your kinsman was your benefactor. He

was good to your father. He arranged for him to do the work of a contractor when his trade went down. That was the year after the one in which you went to the white man's country. Your father did not know the work but Simeon your kinsman taught him and showed him how to make much profit. That was how he was able to send money to you to pay for your education in the white man's country.'

Titus was startled at what his mother was saying. So his father was a contractor when he was in England, and he knew nothing about it!

'Then he died,' she continued sobbing. 'And when he died everything became difficult. I did my best but there's a limit to what a mere woman can do. I could not find the money to send to you for your education.'

'And then what happened, Mother?' he asked, apprehensive.

'He gave me the money, I mean your kinsman Simeon. First he gave me £120. Then after you wrote for more money he gave me another £55. Then just before you came back he gave me £60 for my own trading. He told me not to pay back the first £120. But I'm to pay back the £55 and the £60.'

They were both silent for a moment, mother and son, before she continued: 'That's why you must not go to court to give evidence against your kinsman our benefactor. You now know that you must not do anything against him. If you give evidence against him the Judge will send him to prison. Listen to me, Titus, you are my son, whatever you may become. I carried you on my back and suckled you on these breasts when you were a baby. You must not go to the court to give evidence against your kinsman the Foreman. You must not throw him into prison – I am afraid of the curse of the Oluokun stream, my son. I am afraid of Oluode, your ancestral spirit. You must listen to me. Leave Simeon Oke alone, my son.'

For the next few days Titus lived a living death in Ibala. He did his work mechanically. All Ibala now talked of the impending case. Simeon had since been interdicted and placed on half-pay. Before he went to see his mother Titus had already written his statement for the Police. In it he had confirmed the obvious, that P.W.D. labourers were not allowed to work on a private farm during official working hours. He admitted knowing two or three labourers alleged to have been found on Simeon's farm and confirmed they were P.W.D. labourers. Finally he admitted knowing Simeon Oke and confirmed he was an official of the P.W.D. He now saw that without Simeon's fiddling of P.W.D. business, his own father might never have been able to support him in Britain.

Then Bimpe came to see him. He noticed that she was not accompanied by Chris. He thought he understood why. 'Auntie Bimp, it's a surprise to see you these days,' he said humourlessly.

'But why do you say that, D.E.?' she asked.

'I'm sure you understand.'

'I do not understand,' she said simply. 'And why won't you say good morning to me instead of arguing with me, D.E.? I want a cigarette.'

He took out his case and offered her a cigarette. As he lit it for her he saw that in spite of his resolution to cut her out of his life he still liked her.

'Auntie Bimp, I must ask you to tell me the true relationship between you and the Foreman. You did not tell me that he was more than an acquaintance to you.'

She laughed but did not say anything.

'But you must tell me the truth,' he insisted.

'You don't mean that you did not know that Simeon is the father of my daughter Tola?' she asked simply.

'You have a child for Simeon Oke?' he exclaimed. And yet you—' he did not know how to end the sentence.

'D.E., I'm worried about the things that are going on. And that's why I've come. I don't like the way people are talking about you. I want you to work with me in clearing all the mess we are in.'

'Auntie Bimp, I wish I had known you had a child for Simeon. People thought I knew. Some people have now accused me of wanting to take you from him.'

She looked away from him in an attempt to hide her confusion.

'This is a very serious matter. Some people have suggested that not only am I responsible for the rumoured transfer of Simeon but that I was doing so on account of you – that I want him to be transferred to a distant place that I may have complete access to you.'

'And am I not worth doing that for?'

'Auntie Bimp!' he was surprised at her reaction to the allegation. 'And I know they all now conclude I sent the Police after him.'

The telephone rang. 'Yes, D.E. Ibala. This is the District Engineer. No. I'm afraid I do not employ technical assistants by telephone. You send in a proper application stating your qualifications and experience.' He banged the receiver.

'I know you didn't send the Police after him. Don't worry about that. What people are saying is that you refused to bail him out of custody.'

'Oh dear. And they accuse me of that too!'

'But I know the truth. The Senior Superintendent of Police has told me that you must not stand bail for another civil servant. But, D.E., you know why I've come? I want you to co-operate with me fully. S.S.P. has told me all the things we must do to save the Foreman. It all lies with you. I've seen those that matter.'

'You have! and what must I do?' he asked.

'D.E., that statement you made to the Police. We must withdraw it.'

'Withdraw the statement!'

'I've already told S.S.P. He will do it if you agree. And when the case is taken in court, you must be away in hospital. Then you will not be available to give evidence.'

He looked at her blankly for a moment. He then shook his head and said: 'If a statement is withdrawn surely another can be made—'

'You will make another one – a good one this time.'

'A good one – that will say that all the things that I know are true, are no longer true and that those I know are false are no longer false. Just what d'you think I am, my God!'

'Lawyer has warned me that you will argue. You argue too much, D.E. You must do what we all suggest. And, D.E., let me tell you something: One man alone does not stand against all the world.'

*

Sunmonu the medicine man prepared Simeon for the battle to come. Simeon was aware of what Pastor Morakinyo and the church congregation were doing on his behalf. He also knew that Bimpe and a host of friends were seeing everyone that was anyone in Ibadan about him. But he alone went to Sunmonu the medicine man. And he went at cockcrow, a time of day that both Sunmonu and the god for which he was priest were known to be most alert.

Old Sunmonu gave him two kinds of bath-soap. He was to use the first kind once a day for seven days. In that time all traces of ill-luck would be washed away, and he was sure to win the impending case. The other kind was to be used for washing his face only, and that starting on the day the court began to sit. Whoever he looked at after using that soap would be confused in his thought and in his evidence if such evidence was directed against him. He gave him a series of other things and taught him how to use them. He taught him what incantations he was to recite.

When an elephant walks over a hard-rock outcrop,
We do not see his footprints.
When a buffalo walks over a hard-rock outcrop,
We do not see his footprints.
When a heavy rain falls over a hard-rock outcrop,
We do not see the footprints of the rain.
This was the oracular pronouncement given to Orunmila,
When his enemy full of envy and hate against him,
Said that they were bent on thwarting his honours increase.
But Orunmila said that as for his own affairs,
They were bound to increase his honour continually.
The monkey leaps forward ever, backward never.
The ram charges forward ever, backward never.
As for my enemies on the right hand-side,
Victory over them shall be mine.
What of my enemies in secret?
O Almighty One, give me victory over them, O Supreme
    Deity.
What of my enemies lurking like beasts of prey?
O Almighty One, give me victory over them, O Supreme
    Deity.
All the projects that I undertake
Shall doubtless prosper.

Eighteen

———————◆———————

TITUS was brought back to consciousness by the droning of an engine up the drive. He looked through the window and saw that it was a station wagon. He picked up *The Times* that he had been reading before he dozed off on the couch.

'You in, D.E.?' Ian McLapperton said, pushing open the door.

'Welcome, Scotsman,' Titus said in a voice charged with sleep. He rose to welcome him. 'You didn't tell me you were coming this way today, Ian?'

'No, I didn't,' he said. 'And may I sit down?' he asked and proceeded to sit down without waiting for an answer. 'Passing through to Oshogbo to see how they are getting on with the vote – there appears to be some trouble between Headquarters and Akure. Old Dick is in a temper over the whole thing.'

'Yes, he is,' Titus said. 'He appears to be in a temper over many things. I received the second reminder from him today over some silly accident case. But have a drink. Whisky and soda?'

He asked for beer. As Thomas was fetching it Ian McLapperton looked at his host ominously. He had sniffed the air twice. Titus understood. The scent of a woman's perfume hung heavily in the air. 'I'm not hiding any woman in the cupboard, man. For your information Auntie Bimp and Chris Daniels were here for lunch and have only just gone.'

They talked shop as the visitor drank his beer. He himself drank squash topped up with beer.

Ian McLapperton introduced the delicate subject of the interdiction of Simeon and the pending case. 'It must be very hard for you, the things the boys are saying about you at the All Races.'

'The usual story that I reported the case to the Police and that I insist on coming to give evidence. I suppose it can't be worse than that.'

'The boys are all working hard to stop the case getting to court. Auntie Bimp directs the operations. She has long legs, as you say in this place.'

'And she's using them in the service of Simeon. You know she has a child by Simeon?'

'Of course, I do. Everyone does.'

'You knew that,' Titus said, surprised. 'I did not. I wonder no one warned me.'

'Oh, I thought you knew. It didn't matter really. Besides, no missis to make any palaver.'

They were both silent. Titus lit a cigarette as his visitor poured for himself his second glass of beer. Titus knew that Ian lived with an African girl. He was a married man, his Scottish wife living in Dundee. He'd told him the story once of the doctors in Ibadan having advised that his wife's constitution could not stand the hot humid climate and how she had had to be carted home on an Elder Dempster Lines boat after seven months of illness. That was nine months before her husband was due to complete his first tour of service. McLapperton loved the climate and the people. He certainly loved the girl that deputized for the real Mrs McLapperton. Titus recalled all this background and forgave him his rather lax attitude.

'Ian, you are so different from McBain. That fellow is inhuman. Sees everything in terms of Civil Service Code and Financial Instructions.'

'Not a true Scotsman. His people came originally from England.' They both laughed. 'That reminds me about the accident case you mentioned.'

'I inspected a lorry sent here by the Superintendent of Police. You know the usual routine inspection for roadworthiness.'

'I heard about it – at the All Races.'

'At the All Races of all places!'

In between sips of his drink he told the story. Apparently Titus Oti, the black District Engineer, had angered the Police. He was accused of being arrogant. His education was supposed to have gone into his head. The Police thought that he was too impatient with them and intolerant of their mistakes. They conspired to teach him sense. McLapperton had been in the country for five years and he knew many things including how dangerous the Police could be if one got into their black books.

'While the Police knew that you had tested and certified roadworthy passenger lorry No. CP 457 only a few weeks before the accident they also knew that the cause of accident was neither negligence nor improper conduct on your part, D.E. It was due to the simple fact that only a mere fraction of what you inspected and certified roadworthy was on the road on the day of the accident.'

'How d'you mean? Only a fraction on the road? Where in heaven's name was the other fraction?'

The Scotsman had another sip of his whisky and soda.

'The other fraction? At the outfitters, my boy.'

Titus shook his head.

'You don't understand. I don't blame you. It's like this. The day you tested the lorry you saw five tyres. Four on the lorry and one spare. The spare was brand new. So were two of the four on the wheels. The other two were not new, but they were not old enough to be condemned. The treads were still good.'

Titus nodded. He wondered how McLapperton knew these details which he had himself forgotten.

'The tyres that were seen on the lorry after the accident were all worn out, including the spare.'

'You don't mean it!'

'Yes, my boy. The handbrake on the accident lorry was completely useless. But the handbrake you inspected was in perfect condition.'

'Yes?'

'Yes, the headlamps, the rear light, the speedometer, everything was in perfect condition when you inspected and gave it the roadworthiness certificate.'

'Everything could not have gone wrong in the short space of time between the inspection and the accident.'

'Quite right. But everything except the chassis went back to *Safe Transport Limited*.'

'*Safe Transport Limited*. I've heard of that before.'

'You have indeed. In connection with the legitimate side of its running a normal transport business. Puts two or three regular lorries on the road. But strips down another two lorries for the other, shadier side of his business.'

'Yes?'

'Any lorry going in for a roadworthiness test first goes to the *Safe Transport* workshops. It sheds all its defective parts which are replaced with borrowed parts belonging to *Safe Transport*.'

'And after the test?' Titus asked, understanding dawning on him.

'Quite simple. The borrowed parts go back to *Safe Transport*.'

Titus whistled.

'*Safe Transport Limited* started business with two lorries. When one broke down beyond repair the idea occurred to S.T.L. that he might make more money from the dead horse than he did from the horse when it lived. And he went from strength to strength. In addition to the two lorries stripped down he has a large stock of spares, both for sale and for hire, but mostly for hire.'

'And the Police – what are they doing about it?'

'Just now, nothing. Eighteen months ago they tried to do something. They took *Safe Transport Limited* to court. He was defended by one of your clever lawyers. The prosecution got muddled up in their case. The Magistrate gave them such a dressing-down before he threw out the case.'

'I see.'

'And since then *Safe Transport Limited* has gone from strength to strength.'

'But just one thing, Ian. Who owns *Safe Transport Limited*?'

'Mr Sulaiman originally owned it. But Simeon has come into the business in the last two years.'

'My Foreman even in that racket!'

'Difficult to tell the exact proportion of shareholding. Thanks for the drink.'

Titus wondered if Ian McLapperton was safe to be trusted with his own car. His visitor appeared to be able to read his mind. 'Don't worry about the car. I understand the old horse best when I'm tight. Eighty-three thousand miles. Still going strong.'

Nineteen

———————◇———————

TITUS found himself in a most embarrassing situation. He could not get over the shock of his mother's association with Simeon while he was away in Britain. He was haunted by the thought that most or all of his final year expenses at College in Britain had been financed from money stolen by his kinsman. He considered this a great degradation. He was sure all Ibala knew it. He was also sure that all Ibala knew that when his father was a contractor just before he died his association with his kinsman the Foreman couldn't have been honest. He was not very much worried about this because he knew that the society in which his father lived and died did not consider any acts of dishonesty against Government wrong. Government was an impersonal organization not endowed with the sense of feeling and was therefore incapable of feeling any crimes committed against it and any wrongs done to it. He wondered why he had not come across official traces of his father's short career as a contractor – copies of contract requisitions and payment vouchers.

The knowledge of his indebtedness to Simeon did not make his dislike for his kinsman any less. On the contrary, his pride had been wounded by the fact that the rogue had seen far more of the nakedness of his family than was good for a subordinate or even a colleague of equal standing. He was certain that sooner or later Simeon would use all this to blackmail him. A most embarrassing situation for anyone to be in.

His mother had become completely intolerable in the way she brought pressure on him not to go to court to give evidence against Simeon. She was incapable of understanding that he was completely helpless in the matter and that the decision was in the hands of the law officers and the Police. He had no doubt that powerful influences were already working in favour of Simeon in that direction and indeed in the direction of killing the case entirely. He remembered Bimpe, and sighed.

Then he decided to get away from it all at least for a few days. He therefore arranged a tour of the Division. He would go from Ibala to Igbetti, from Igbetti to Iseyin and back to Ibala.

He was fascinated by the excellent country through which he was motoring. Unlike the dense heavy forest country around Ibala the vegetation here in the approaches to Igbetti was the typical savanna of the Middle Belt of Nigeria – tall grass with a few trees with thick bark and of stunted growth. He was intrigued to see a huge baboon crossing the road some fifty yards ahead. He slowed down when he got to the spot and watched with interest the back view of the retreating beast. But a few moments later he saw a still greater spectacle, a whole family of monkeys, easily a dozen, crossing the road this time some hundred yards ahead. He pressed hard on his accelerator that he might reach the spot before the last of them crossed the road. He was absolutely fascinated. This was the true Africa of the dream of the European and the American, where man and monkey fought for space, under the watchful eye of the elephant and the lion.

He stopped at the old rest-house, and while Thomas was getting his lunch ready he decided to climb the famous rock. It offered a splendid view from the rest-house, the grey rock with clusters of green here and there where some persistent tree had taken advantage of decaying leaves in a rock crevice in which to force its roots in spite of all handicaps.

The rest-house caretaker, himself a native of Igbetti, offered to take him to the top of the rock. There he was fascinated by what he saw: ruins of houses in mud-wall construction. He remembered having read an article in the popular *Nigeria* magazine about how the Igbettis had fled before the invading Fulani warriors from Northern Nigeria during the inter-tribal wars and scampered up the rock. There on the flat top they had built houses and lived for a long time while the Fulani invasion lasted. Here, then, he was reading history as recorded on the rock. He was thrilled at the ruined houses and broken pots and hollows dug out of the face of the rock in which the people had ground corn and pepper. At the edge of the rock in one area he saw a number of rock chunks precariously balanced, ready to be rolled down the face of the rock. These had been placed in this position by the defenders of the Igbetti of old. They were rolled down the face of the rock on to the Fulani horsemen who, according to history, attempted to ride their horses up the rock to meet the Igbetti defenders. The Igbettis did eventually come down to their town at the foot of the rock many months after the Fulanis had withdrawn. But they left the rock chunks in position at the top of the rock, ready at a moment's notice to be catapulted down the rock face if ever the Fulanis came again.

As for monkeys he saw plenty of them. He had his twelve-bore with him but he took the advice of the caretaker not to shoot any monkeys on the rock as, according to him, he had known a case where an English District Officer had been attacked and caned by a herd of angry monkeys after he had shot one of them – on that same rock.

Back at the rest-house he felt quite tired, and he attacked his lunch with a good appetite. Half-way through it he heard his boy Thomas arguing with someone on the verandah. The squeaking of cocks and the bleating of a goat made it impossible for him to hear what was going on. But Thomas told him later. The *Bale* had sent greetings to the District Engineer and would be pleased if he would call on him before proceeding on his journey. He had sent a goat, two cocks and a bottle of gin as a token of respect. Titus knew that not to accept the gifts and not to call to see the old man would be interpreted as an insult and a sign of disrespect.

Motoring down to the *Bale*'s compound he raised a large dust-storm, and attracted a large crowd of children. After parking his car outside, he paused to admire the architecture of the entrance to the compound. He was interested in the sculptured timber posts that supported the eaves of the roof on the verandah.

Inside, the old *Bale* and his chiefs received him. He was made to sit on a high-backed chair next to the *Bale* on the dais. The chiefs sat on chairs and benches at the foot of the dais, and in the rest of the hall.

After he had sat down one of the men rose to make a formal tedious speech of welcome in English, spiced with irrelevant passages from Shakespeare and from the Scriptures. He told the District Engineer that they in Igbetti were illustrious people and they did not want to take a back seat in the group of towns in the District. That was why they had called him as a God-fearing man to construct for them a waterworks, a hospital, a town hall and good roads.

Titus said a few words in Yoruba. He would do his best, but all depended not on him but on the Resident and the District Officer and the Provincial Engineer. He would let those others know what the Igbetti people wanted, as soon as he was back at Ibala.

'But you have not said anything about the other engineer, Mr Simeon Oke. He has not been good to us.'

Titus was taken aback by the *Bale*'s remarks. In this somewhat remote area people did not think much of his kinsman the Foreman.

'He is not a good man,' the *Bale* continued. 'He has done many things wrong here. He deceived us. We do not like people who deceive us.'

'That man dare not show his face here again in this town,' one of the chiefs said. 'He abducted the wife of my son. The day he comes here again, he dies.'

Titus just managed to get back to the rest-house before a terrific storm came. He stood on the verandah watching the trees struggling in the storm and he pondered on the mighty force of air in motion. He was warned by the caretaker to avoid staying on the verandah while it was raining as Sango the god of thunder did not like it and might send lightning to kill him. Titus remembered having read that Igbetti was prone to serious thunderstorms and the incidence of death by lightning there was quite high.

After the storm he set out from Igbetti. But great disappointment awaited him seven miles away. The concrete culvert over a stream that had flooded during the storm had been completely washed away and it was absolutely impossible to get across. He returned to the rest-house. He told the caretaker what had happened and of his intention to stay the night in the rest-house.

'Master wants to sleep in Igbetti Rest House?' the caretaker asked in the greatest astonishment.

'Of course, yes. And I want you to get the place ready. But before you do that I want you to send for the road overseer.'

'I shall go for the road overseer. But I beg master not to sleep in the rest-house.'

'Why?'

'Master, I just beg you not to sleep here, that is all.'

Titus did not understand the nonsense the caretaker was talking, and he did not want to give much thought to it. After the caretaker had gone to look for the overseer he walked round the grounds of the rest-house. He admired the tall cassia trees and the frangipani. There were great clusters of bougainvillaea. The Pride of Barbados had grown somewhat wild. He came suddenly upon a stone monument, just visible in the thick grass that had overgrown the area. He went nearer. A tombstone without doubt. With the butt of his gun he beat aside the tall blades of grass that he might be able to read the inscription on the brass plate. He read: 'Sacred to the memory of Captain Henry James, District Commissioner in the Yoruba Country. Died mysteriously at Igbetti, 14 July 1905.'

He heard a hiss, and he saw some movement in the grass a few feet away from him. Then he saw a huge black snake. He stood rooted to the spot. But at that moment the snake made away effortlessly through the grass, passing very near him. Having regained his senses he himself fled.

14 July! That was the date he had read on the tombstone. 14 July 1905. What a most curious coincidence, he thought, for the day he was visiting the rest-house was 14 July It was most strange that he should be paying his first visit to the rest-house on the anniversary of the death of Captain Henry James, possibly in the very grounds of the rest-house.

The overseer was waiting for him. His greetings were very tedious, as was customary with the people of these parts. How was Madam? How were the children? Did D.E. have a pleasant journey from Ibala? Did the caretaker truly take care of D.E.?

Titus came to the point. Culvert No. 7/2 on the Igbetti–Igboho Road had been washed away. The overseer should arrange a proper night watch with red lamps on both sides of the stream to warn traffic.

The overseer told him he would carry out his instructions immediately. He, however, had a very important matter to discuss with the D.E. He said he understood that the D.E. intended to stay the night at Igbetti. He had made suitable arrangements in the town for his accommodation.

'But I intend to stay here in the rest-house.'

'Allah forbid that D.E. should sleep in the rest-house. You are welcome in my own house. I have an iron bed, and I've already bought a good mattress for your use. You will be quite comfortable. I have also arranged for a mosquito net.'

Titus regarded the grand old man with interest. He imagined himself sleeping in a windowless room and probably suffocating to death at night. No doubt the old man had gone into much trouble to arrange for his accommodation. But his decision must be obvious. He could not accept the overseer's offer. He told him so and instructed him to proceed with the arrangements for the night watch at the damaged culvert.

He set out on another walk, this time down the drive while his steward Thomas got his things out ready for the night – the camp-bed and mosquito net – and drinks. Half-way down the drive he noticed a procession of people coming up. He wondered if they were men looking for contracts or wanting to be engaged as road labourers.

Wherever he went he was always haunted by people who wanted things for themselves or for their relatives.

He recognized the most important in the group as someone he had seen earlier on at the meeting he held in the *Bale*'s compound. After exchanging the usual courtesies the head-man told him that they had brought greetings and an important message from the *Bale*. The *Bale* understood that he intended to stay the night in Igbetti. He was pleased to hear this and had invited him to stay in his compound. He should come down in his car and inspect his house. He was welcome to any of the many rooms in it. He should come down to indicate which of them he wanted and it would be fitted to his satisfaction.

He was getting worried that so many people were now showing interest in his night arrangements. He was certain a night at the *Bale*'s would be worse than at his overseer's house. He bade the chief greet the *Bale* and thank him for his offer but regretted that he could not accept it as he was already comfortably settled in the rest-house.

'But you must not sleep in the rest-house,' one of the men said. 'It is dangerous.'

'Ghosts, Engineer,' the chief said.

'Ghosts,' he said. 'I'm not afraid of ghosts.'

'Ghosts. Real ghosts, Engineer. Do not sleep in the rest-house. Even Europeans run away from this rest-house.'

They could not persuade him. So they left him both disappointed and worried. Later in the evening the road-overseer came back ostensibly to inform him that he had carried out his instructions in respect of the washed-out culvert but in reality to implore him to change his mind about sleeping in the haunted house. He went near him and squatted as a sign of respect as he invoked the name of Allah and of Mohammed his Prophet to make him change his mind.

But Titus did not change his mind.

When the old overseer bade him good night he knew he really meant good-bye as he never expected that he would ever again see him alive.

Twenty

⸻ ◇ ⸻

HE changed into his night clothes and, sitting in one of the four easy chairs, tried to read himself to sleep with Somerset Maugham's *Of Human Bondage*, aided with a double whisky. The light from the Tilley-lamp was quite strong and attracted a large number of winged ants of the species that breed in large numbers after a shower of rain. They were a perfect nuisance. When he felt ready to go to bed he put out the light, took out the torch and checked the bolts of the doors.

He must have been dozing for some time when suddenly he sniffed the air. There was no mistaking the thing, a very strong smell of tobacco. He had not smoked at all that day – he was for the third time attempting to give up smoking. Must be Thomas his steward, he at first concluded. But he was in the boys' quarters, a considerable distance away. There was no doubt about it. He was convinced someone was around. He lay still in bed.

After some time the tobacco smell disappeared. He heaved a sigh of relief. He thought he had been imagining things. He thought he must have been influenced by the silly story of the overseer and the caretaker about the rest-house being haunted. He tried to sleep. But hard as he tried sleep just wouldn't come. After some time he got up and decided to continue reading. He tried to light the lamp, but he couldn't do it. He shouted for Thomas but no sound came from the boys' quarters. He cursed him. No doubt he'd sneaked into town to seek prostitutes. He was no Yoruba and would not be able to speak their language. But the language of sex was universal and made easy with the dictionary of money, in the transaction from a willing buyer to an equally willing seller. There was a hurricane lantern. He knew where the box of matches was and so he lit the lamp and continued reading in the poorer light.

Then it came again, the tobacco smell. His head appeared to swell gradually to double, then triple and indeed to four times the normal size. There was something wrong with him inside. He rose to his feet, unsteadily. 'Who's that?' he shouted. There was no reply. He carried the lantern and went round the house, from the bedroom to the sitting-room and then to the dining-room. He saw nothing that he had not seen before.

Once more the tobacco smell disappeared. His head returned to its normal weight. He came back to resume his reading. He convinced himself that he was being silly.

But it came a third time, that tobacco smell, stronger and quicker than before. And what was more this time it was accompanied by someone whistling *Men of Harlech*. Titus sat absolutely still, frightened to death. After *Men of Harlech* the whistler embarked upon *Poor Old Joe*. In the middle of it the whistling stopped rather suddenly.

'Who's that?' Titus cried. He hurried out of the chair and looked for his gun. He made for the door and unbolted it fast. He got to the verandah and fired a shot into the innocent sky. 'Whoever you are I dare you to come out here, if you're man enough. And I assure you there are five other rounds where that one came from.'

Then he went back to his chair after bolting the door behind him. He steadied his nerves with another double whisky. Good old whisky. What would the world be without whisky? He convinced himself once more that he was just being silly, imagining things. He was not afraid of ghosts. There were no ghosts.

Not afraid of ghosts? What about Simeon his kinsman? But was Simeon a ghost? Surely he wasn't dead and therefore could not be a ghost. Then he became confused. Was Simeon not dead? Did he Titus not attend the funeral a few days back? That was it. Simeon was dead. It was the ghost of the rascal that had been torturing him. But, but, but Simeon was not dead, he was certain. Then he became hopelessly confused and frightened. He thought that he had gone mad.

And then it came again, the tobacco smell. And more than whistling came with it this time. He saw the strange man through the window, coming up the drive. The moon was just coming out and he could not see the details of his face or his dress. He might be an Englishman or a Syrian, but he did not look like an African. He appeared to be in a tight-fitting military uniform. And he wore a helmet – in the night!

Titus seized his gun. 'Stop, or I fire,' he shouted in an unsteady voice. The man coming up the drive did stop. Titus regained some confidence. Apparently this was no ghost who would not have been frightened by his threat of firing. It was understandable that rogues and beggars should take advantage of the belief of the local population that the rest-house was haunted to use it for unlawful purposes.

'Stay where you are,' he said, covering the stranger

with his gun. 'Tell me who you are, and what you want here.'

Apparently that angered the strange man of Igbetti. For he charged up the drive.

'Stop, I warn you,' Titus shouted. The man did not stop.

'Stop, or I fire,' Titus shouted; his self-assurance had once more evaporated. But the man of Igbetti ignored his warning.

'If you take one more step, you die,' he issued a final warning. He leant against the wall to steady himself. Still the stranger continued in his menacing course up the drive.

Then he fired one shot over his head, and hoped, and prayed to God that that would show the stranger that he meant business. He now truly meant business. He must now shoot to kill. For the way the stranger came up the drive with determined steps convinced him he meant no good. This was going to be the last fight for him or for his unwelcome visitor.

He saw him board the concrete pavement of the verandah. He aimed at his neck and fired. But the man continued to come. He saw him walk past the bolted door – Good Lord! He was now only a few yards from him. He shouted for Thomas. He shouted for his mother. He shouted for his fiancée Bola in England. He shouted for everybody that was anybody that he could remember. He fired his gun in all directions. Then he fell senseless on the floor.

Twenty-one

---◇---

THE following afternoon Deborah created a scene at the hospital at Ibadan where her son Titus lay delirious in a special ward. The story had reached Ibala early in the morning that the District Engineer had had a strange encounter at Igbetti and that he had gone quite mad. Another version of the story said that it was true that he had gone mad and was already in chains at the lunatic asylum in Ibadan. He had not died, all versions of the story agreed on that. So Pastor Morakinyo, Deborah and other well-wishers and gossip-mongers from Ibala hurried by lorry to Ibadan.

When Deborah entered the hospital the gateman told her she could not pass as she had not come at the official visiting hour.

'But I must pass. I've got to take him back home with me.'

'Who are you taking back home with you?' the gateman asked, proud in his khaki uniform.

'Titus, my son; I want to take him away from here.' And she brushed past him. But he held her by her *iborun*, which promptly came off. 'Come back, woman,' he cried. 'You won't go if even you have a dozen sons here.'

By this time a crowd had formed round Deborah and the gateman. 'You can insult me as much as you like. But I'm going to take him away from here,' she said crossing her arms over her bosom in motherly determination. While the crowd continued to grow and while most of them were enlightening her about hospital discipline and procedure, Pastor Morakinyo came out of the male ward.

'Sister Deborah is the mother of Engineer Titus,' he explained to the gateman. 'Engineer Titus is in the special ward.'

'I respect you, Reverend. But regardless of who her son is she must wait till visiting hours. That's the order.'

'But I must remove him now,' Deborah repeated, determined.

'Remove him?' Pastor Morakinyo repeated, darkly. 'You cannot remove him. The doctor says he must not be disturbed at all.'

'Pastor, he's my son, and not yours. I'm going to move him. They say he's mad. There's no madness in the history of my family, nor in the family of his father.'

A nursing sister came out and called for silence. She threatened to report the gateman to the doctor for his failure to keep out trouble-makers.

'You see my trouble now?' the gateman cried in appeal to all around. 'All of you, you hear her? Do you not all see how I've been telling this woman, this witch, to go away? Now Sister wants to report me to Doctor. You see my trouble!'

'He calls me witch,' Deborah cried. 'You all hear him? Pastor, you hear him? He calls me witch – this dog.'

'Sister Deborah, please,' Pastor Morakinyo remonstrated with her.

'You all hear him, this bastard, this—'

'Deborah, please.'

She charged the luckless gateman, held the lapels of his coat and was about to slap him before he was rescued from her. There was confusion.

Then, Simeon appeared on the scene. He too appealed to her to listen to reason. She looked at him for a brief moment. She sized him up, in the contemptuous way only women know how to. Then she said: 'You are here too, Simeon. You follow him here to the hospital. You could not complete your objective of killing him at Igbetti. Now you follow him here.'

'Sister Deborah!' Pastor Morakinyo cried.

'Pastor, I must speak my mind,' she cried. 'He has been going to make *juju* from old Sunmonu. Yes, you Simeon, I know it all. You will have to kill me first. And, and—'

'Sister Deborah! Brother Simeon, please don't answer her. Do move away from here,' Pastor Morakinyo entreated.

'And one thing I shall tell you, Simeon – the bone of my son, and my own bone will choke you to death. For you will have to kill me first before you can kill him. You will have to eat me first, before you can eat him. That's all.'

But that was not all, unfortunately. For when the doctor came and was being accorded the respect and courtesies that are usually extended to doctors, Deborah continued to shout that she wanted to remove her son and that she was sure his kinsman Simeon would kill him if she was not allowed to remove him. When the doctor explained that the District Engineer must not be moved she retorted – 'And you call yourself a doctor. Just what do you know is wrong with my son?'

'He's gravely ill.'

'Yes, but you don't know anything about witchcraft,

do you? He is suffering from witchcraft. And it is this wicked man Simeon that has done it. He has made Sunmonu the *juju* man in Ibala put witchcraft on my son. And only the same Sunmonu can cure him. The white man's medicine cannot cure him.'

After some whispered conversation with Pastor Morakinyo the doctor declared that he was prepared to release the patient to the native doctor who could cure him of witchcraft – but not to her. She should go and fetch Sunmonu.

The trick worked. She set out for Ibala, bent on persuading Sunmonu to follow her back to Ibadan to claim from the hospital doctor the patient that only he could cure, but whom the ethics of the medical profession prevented from being delivered by the hospital doctor to his layman relatives.

But at Ibala Deborah fell ill, very ill.

Pastor Morakinyo expressed anxiety over Deborah's illness. She had refused to go to hospital. But Pa Joel had a strange explanation of her illness. 'You know, Pastor,' he said, seriously, 'there is something I have been meaning to tell you for some time. Deborah is a witch.'

'Sister Deborah is a witch?' Pastor Morakinyo said in astonishment.

'Yes, I've been meaning to tell you this for a long time. But then I've been hesitating, not knowing how you would react to it. I know that you, Pastor, ridicule a number of things which you think are foolish just because the white man does not understand them. But in spite of your being a Pastor you are still an African. You cannot pretend not to know how serious it is for someone to be a witch. Deborah is a witch.'

'But Elder Joel, how can you say this?'

'Pastor, it is because Deborah is a witch that all these

terrible things are happening to her. First her husband Samuel died.'

'But, Elder Joel, we all knew what killed Elder Samuel.'

'Deborah did. Samuel, my late brother's son, was killed by Deborah his own wife. Pastor, my late brother's son was a good man. When he wanted to marry Deborah we all objected in the family, for we knew the mother of Deborah was a witch. We did not want our son to marry the daughter of a witch. Then Samuel was overcome by the witchcraft of Deborah's mother. He became leaner and leaner. So we consulted the Ifa priest who confirmed our fears and told us that if Samuel did not marry Deborah her mother's witchcraft would surely kill him. He taught us what to do to neutralize the effect of the witchcraft – we did it and Deborah's mother died shortly after.'

Pastor Morakinyo continued to listen to the story, without indicating whether or not he believed it.

'We did not know that her mother had passed the witchcraft on to Deborah before she died, till she killed her husband Samuel.'

'But, Elder, as a Christian you cannot believe these things.'

'Pastor, you are now practically a member of our family. That is why I'm telling you these things. Deborah's witchcraft which killed her husband has affected her son, Titus.'

'Yes, Elder?'

'Do you not see the way he's been behaving since he came back from the white man's country? It is his mother's witchcraft that has affected his brain. And now both mother and son are lying ill. I tell you it's all the woman's witchcraft. But, Pastor, I will tell you something, I'm going to see someone who is stronger than she is in witchcraft. I'm not going to see her kill the son of my brother's son so easily.'

For the rest of the day Pastor Morakinyo reflected on this strange story. Elder Joel and all the church folk believed in witchcraft and in *juju*. The old man had been frank with him. He'd confessed to going to the Ifa priest for professional consultation on matters beyond his immediate comprehension. Morakinyo sighed as he recollected that that was what most of his congregation did. They attended the church twice on Sunday and bible class once during the week. They prayed to God twice a day asking for this and that. But they secretly went to the Ifa priest and the Sango priest at night to ask for the intercession of the gods in matters for which their Christian faith did not appear to have an immediate answer.

Morakinyo prayed for the restoration of Deborah and of Titus to good health. He prayed for Brother Simeon to be freed in the case pending in court. He prayed for peace in the church and in Ibala. And he prayed for all sorts and condition of men, that it might please God to comfort and relieve them according to their several necessities, giving them patience in their sufferings and a happy issue out of their afflictions.

The mystery of the strange experience of Titus at the Igbetti rest-house deepened with Deborah's illness. It was Simeon who had conveyed him to hospital in his old Prefect car. He explained at the hospital that he had received a message from the road overseer at Igbetti that, in spite of all advice, the District Engineer had insisted on sleeping at the Igbetti rest-house. He had hurried to Igbetti to see if he could not persuade him to change his mind. He had hoped that he would arrive in Igbetti before it was too late. But according to him he did arrive too late. On arrival he called the overseer. The caretaker absolutely refused to join the party, that he was certain was courting sure death. When the car drew up at the drive of the rest-house Simeon and his companion saw no sign of life, except for the bush lantern which was burning low. Simeon shouted the name of the District Engineer. There was no reply. He shouted for Thomas. Thomas had come out of the boys' quarters as soon as he saw Simeon's car driving up the drive. Simeon asked him where his master was. He told the visitor that he was already in bed and did not wish to be disturbed as he had a very tiring day. But, as he was speaking, the overseer shouted and pulled the sleeve of Simeon's jumper, pointing at something with his free hand. Both Simeon and Thomas followed the direction he indicated. Then they both saw what he had seen. They saw Titus sprawled on the floor near one of the chairs, with his gun at his side.

Twenty-two

———————◇———————

THE prosecution found it difficult to collect evidence against Simeon Oke, particularly in respect of his claiming mileage allowance and actually receiving payment in respect of his car known to have been laid up for three and a half months. No one was willing to come forward to give evidence. 'You are wasting your time if you think that my man will come to court to give evidence against Mr Oke,' an overdressed girl with heavy make-up told the C.I.D. officer over a glass of Star beer at the All Races Club. 'Just why won't you people leave the Foreman alone?'

'Can you help us, sir, about the car?' the policeman asked the clubman, ignoring his girl-friend.

'Help you do what – get Simeon Oke into trouble?' the man asked, sipping his stout.

'No, sir. We just want to know if you saw Car No. CL 457 laid up here for several days together. That is all we want to know, sir. Nothing to do with going to court, sir.'

'No. We did not see the car,' the girl spoke for her boy-friend. 'We do not watch details of the cars that come in and go out of the club. And you want to know why?'

The police officer looked at her without saying anything, but certainly interested in why she and her boyfriend didn't watch details of car movements at the club.

'We mind our own business,' she exploded, giving the unfortunate policeman a look that was meant to quell him – a look which only women are capable of giving to those they do not like.

The prosecution eventually decided to drop the two charges of conspiracy to defraud and stealing centred round the idle car. Instead they concentrated on the charges connected with the use of P.W.D. labourers on Simeon's farm.

The case was in the Magistrate's Court in a matter of a couple of months. This was extraordinary in the known circumstances of cases taking a long time before ever getting to the courts, and dragging on for months and months while both the prosecution and the defence counsel prayed for adjournments for this and that reason. It was rumoured that Titus was at the bottom of the expedited hearing. Titus himself thought that the Resident, to whom a copy of the original letter that had led to the police investigations and arrest of Simeon Oke had been sent, was responsible.

The first prosecution witness was one of the two police officers who had arrested the two labourers on the cocoa plantation alleged to be Simeon Oke's. He deposed on oath that as a result of information received he and his colleague went to a cocoa plantation at Mile 7, Ibala–Iwana Road. There they saw the first and second accused working on the plantation. He identified the first two men in the dock as the men he had seen on the farm.

'Working on the plantation,' the Crown Counsel interrupted the witness. 'Were they working with hoes or with matchets? Were they weeding the farm or harvesting cocoa pods? Tell his Worship exactly what you found the first and second accused doing.'

The witness explained what he meant. He went on to say that after disclosing their identities he and his colleague took the first and second accused in their van back to the police station. There they took down their statement, which statements were duly read to them and interpreted to them in the Yoruba language.

'And is this the statement of the first accused?' the Counsel passed on to the witness a sheet of paper marked 'Exhibit Two'. The witness confirmed that it was. The Counsel next passed on to him a similar document marked 'Exhibit Three'. The witness confirmed this was the statement of the second accused. The two documents were passed on to His Worship who adjusted his glasses to read through them. Both accused had stated that they were employees of the P.W.D. and that they had been instructed by their boss, the section-man, to go and work on the farm instead of working on the road. They knew the farm belonged to the foreman, Mr Simeon Oke. They went to work there on instruction. They did not refuse to work there because they never refused the instructions of their section-man.

Chris Daniels, Barrister-at-Law, leading the defence, rose to tell the court that he had no questions to ask the first prosecution witness. This was a surprise to everyone, including the Magistrate, for Chris Daniels was known to hate the police for what he usually called their inefficiency and their barbaric methods in forcing statements out of people under duress. He was notorious for his technique of subjecting police witnesses to much indignity in the witness-box. Today he had no questions to ask of the police officer.

The timekeeper gave evidence next for the prosecution. The Crown Counsel tried to establish through him the case that the two men were regular employees of the P.W.D. and that they ought to have been working on the Ibala–Iwana Road the day they were found working on Simeon Oke's farm. Chris Daniels tried to establish the contrary point that the men were casual labourers, having no binding contract with Government other than an agreement on a day-to-day basis that for every day they turned up and did work on the road they would be entitled to the payment of 2s 7d each. Chris Daniels cited legal authority to prove his point. His Worship took note of the argument of the Defence after shouting 'Silence', and looking sternly round the room at the benches of spectators who were exhibiting their appreciation of Chris Daniels's learning by much whispering and tittering.

At the resumed hearing the following day, the prosecution applied for leave to withdraw the charges against the first two accused. Chris Daniels rose to welcome the action of the prosecution. He congratulated his learned friend, the prosecuting counsel, on seeing reason at last. He pointed out the futility of continuing with the case against Simeon Oke, the third accused. He advised his learned friend not to waste the valuable time of His Worship any longer and to drop the case against Simeon.

But the prosecution did not drop the case against Simeon.

The star witness for the day was Pa Joel. He was led in evidence by Chris Daniels after he had been sworn on the Bible. 'You are Joel Tobatele and you are the head of the Tobatele–Oti family in Ibala?' The Registrar interpreted this into Yoruba.

'I am Joel Tobatele. My elder brother is dead. He was the father of Samuel Oti, the father of Titus Oti. As I am now the oldest man in the family, I am now the father of the family and all the others are—'

'You are the father of the family,' Chris repeated after him, cutting him short. You must answer the questions precisely, Pa Joel. The big judge does not like you to talk too much.' Pa Joel glared at the 'big judge' as if to query his limiting him in the number of words in which he chose to define his status in the family.

'As the head of the family – or the father of the family, can you tell His Worship what your functions are?'

'As head of the family I settle quarrels. Whenever the women quarrel they bring the matter to me. Whenever the men flog their wives they bring the matter to me to settle. And—'

'But, Pa, His Worship the big judge does not want you to tell him about family quarrels. He only—'

'Do you say the big judge does not want to hear about family quarrels?' He asked in astonishment. 'How can he settle the quarrel between Simeon and Titus then?' he asked, staring at the Magistrate. 'Or is it not the quarrel between the two of them we have all come to settle?'

'Perhaps if you ask him what particular function you mean he will understand and give a straightforward answer, Mr Daniels,' the Magistrate observed.

'Most obliged, Your Worship,' Chris said with a sophisticated bow to the Magistrate. 'Look, Pa, as the head of the family, is it you or someone else who has authority over the family land at – what's the name of the family land now— Yes, at Iwana Oko?'

'Look, I have told you once that I am the head of the family. My elder sister is a woman. Does a woman have authority over land – does the man not always have precedence over the woman? Why are you asking me these questions?'

The Magistrate shook his head more in pity than in anger against the rambling old man. The spectators whispered and tittered.

Chris made another attempt 'Look, Pa, the Magistrate does not say that woman has precedence over man. Since this is the case, and since in your family there is no other man older than you, is there someone else who has authority over your family land?'

'I have told you that I am the oldest man in the family. I have authority over the family land, and—'

'You have authority over the family land, Pa. That's all His Worship wants to know from you,' the counsel said, looking up at the Magistrate who was writing down the evidence in his book. 'And did you, as the head of the family, give any land to Simeon Oke? Tell His Worship the big judge. Did you?'

'I did not give any land to Simeon. His father's father was the youngest—'

'Please answer my question, Pa,' Chris said, impatiently. 'Did you, as the head of the family, measure out a piece of your family land and give it to Simeon Oke.'

'How can I give him land? Before I give him land will I not have to call a family meeting and—'

'And did you call a family meeting and after it give him land?'

'No. I did not call any meeting. And I did not give him any land. And—'

'That is all. You did not give him any land. The land on which some people were found working the day the police trespassed on your family farmland was therefore not Simeon's farm.'

'That was not Simeon's farm at all,' the old man laughed aloud in the witness-box. 'That cocoa farm belonged to Samuel, father of Titus. After he died—'

'The farm was Samuel's. Is it Simeon's?'

'The farm is not Simeon's,' the old man said.

'Good, the farm is not Simeon's. The farm belonged to the father of Engineer Titus, that's what you have just said. The farm may well belong to Mr Titus Oti, son of Samuel Oti. And Titus Oti is District Engineer, P.W.D., Ibala,' Chris Daniel said the last words looking out of the window.

'Your Worship, I object to the ugly insinuation of my learned friend,' the prosecuting counsel cried, jumping to his feet. There followed what newspapers usually describe as heated exchanges between the two lawyers. Pa Joel in the witness-box looked from the one to the other, wondering what was the matter with both of them. Eventually the Magistrate observed with a smile that he wondered why both counsel should always engage in such fierce battle before him. It was their duty as members of the learned profession to endeavour through their examination of witnesses to draw out the truth which would assist the court in arriving at a just decision. But counsel took this to mean that the Magistrate had not sustained the objection of the prosecuting counsel, who sat down, surprisingly not disappointed and after he had laughingly said: 'As Your Worship pleases.'

After the Registrar had interpreted the piece about Titus owning the farm on which P.W.D. labourers had been found working, Pa Joel said that Titus was not the owner of the farm. 'I come here to beg you to settle the quarrel between my two children, Simeon and Titus. I am an old man and—'

'Pa, you come here to give evidence in a case where one of your children has been charged with grievous offence which, if proved, may lead him to gaol,' Chris Daniels said, warningly. 'His Worship is not interested in your family quarrels. He cannot settle your quarrels. So keep to the point, and answer only the questions put to you.'

The old man was visibly distressed when the lawyer's observation had been interpreted to him. He opened his mouth in surprise and complete helplessness. He looked at the Magistrate as if to ask, 'Just why are you here then if you will not settle the quarrel between Titus and his kinsman the Foreman?'

The Magistrate was an understanding man and he ruled that the witness should be allowed to say what was in his mind. The old man nodded happily towards the Magistrate after he'd learnt of his ruling.

'The white man has put you in the position of a big judge and an elder,' he said to His Worship. 'You have wisdom like Solomon, son of David,' he continued to the embarrassment of the bar. But His Worship was apparently enjoying the old man's harmless display. 'Both Titus and Simeon are my children. I must not tell lies against either of them. If I do the family god Oluokun will punish me. The god of kindred Ajobi will punish me. That is why I must tell no lie against either Titus or Simeon. Titus is not the owner of the farm we are talking about. He has no interest in farms. That is the truth. I think when he went to the white man's country he has read books beyond the point where people are interested in farms.'

Both bench and bar and the body of the court roared with laughter. Pa Joel himself joined in the laughter, feeling important in being able to lead the whole court in this pleasurable relaxation. 'And I want to tell you something,' he said, after the laughter had subsided a little. 'It is a bad thing for people to learn books beyond the point where they are no longer interested in farms.' That again set the whole court rocking with laughter.

The prosecution counsel cross-examined the witness. He reminded the old man of the importance of telling the truth, the whole truth and nothing but the truth, at all times particularly when one was old and nearing the grave. When he asked the old man if he knew the horrors of hell where people who told lies before the Magistrate would burn for eternity, Chris Daniels jumped to his feet to object to the line that the cross-examination was taking. The Magistrate sustained his objection and advised prosecution counsel to ask only questions relevant to the case.

'As head of the family, you have not given any land to Titus Oti, the District Engineer?' No, he had not. Titus Oti wanted no farmland.

'Titus Oti wanted no farmland. He is unlike some others who had not read books beyond the point where they are no longer interested in farming?'

Yes, that was so. A good number of *alakowes*, in spite of their having been to school and wearing the white man's dress, are still interested in farming.

'Like your favourite child, Simeon Oke. He's interested in lands and in farming?'

Chris Daniels jumped to his feet and roared like a wounded lion. He protested that his learned friend was quite wrong in law to have said what he said and he took every objection to it. This led to another heated exchange between the two lawyers which curiously enough His Worship allowed to run its course. Then he observed that he saw nothing wrong in the observation of the prosecution counsel, who, flushed with victory, repeated his observation.

Yes, Simeon Oke was interested in lands and in farms. And that showed that he was the true son of his father, who was a very famous farmer.

Chris Daniels' face was red. His witness had swallowed the bait of the prosecution counsel, who threw in a further bait.

'Pa, Simeon Oke loves farms. He's a great farmer. So great is his enthusiasm that he could have taken a piece of the farm left by his elder cousin Samuel, without asking for your permission.'

The old man saw this particular bait and did not swallow it. He said that to do that would be stealing family land and Simeon would never do that.

Titus gave his evidence two days after. Led in evidence by the prosecution counsel he confirmed that he was not interested in farms and farmlands. He had no farm and certainly did not instruct any P.W.D. labourers to work on any farm. He did not know whether or not Simeon Oke had any farms. He did not know whether the particular farm on which labourers had been found working belonged to Simeon Oke or not. He confirmed that it would be wrong for P.W.D. labourers to do work on private farms during normal working hours.

Curiously enough, Chris Daniels said he had no questions to ask the witness.

Three days after, the Magistrate discharged and acquitted Simeon Oke. The prosecution, His Worship said in his thirty-five minutes' judgement, had failed to prove the charges against the accused beyond all reasonable doubt that the cocoa farm on which P.W.D. men were found working belonged to the accused. In the circumstances he was discharging and acquitting him. He was, however, directing that a formal letter be written to the Director of Public Works bringing to his notice a number of things revealed at the trial which, to his mind, should be the subject of a departmental inquiry under the Public Service Commission Regulations.

Twenty-three

---◇---

MCBAIN was speaking on the telephone when Titus entered his office. Whilst he waited, Titus busied himself over the charts and tables on the walls of the Provincial Engineer's office. Statistics measuring the progress on the various roads and building projects in all the nine districts in the Province, including Ibala his own district. He noticed that here the expenditure graph was well ahead of the progress graph – another sordid reminder of the activities of his kinsman, the Foreman. He saw what he had already known, that he was the only African on the senior service list of engineers: according to the list he was number fifteen out of an establishment of nineteen.

He was pondering the question of his seniority on the list when McBain dropped the telephone receiver. 'I trust you're getting on fine at Ibala, Mr Oti?' he asked, looking his visitor straight in the face.

'I fear I'm not, Mr McBain,' he said, obviously dejected.

'You're not? I'm sorry to hear that. What's the matter now, Mr Oti? Nothing to do with the time you wasted going to court in the Rex *versus* Simeon Oke and Others case?' he said with a bit of sarcasm.

'It is difficult to forget it. The waste of time, and the humiliation.'

'Why are you worried about that, man? Your time is paid for by Government, my dear Mr Oti. Whether you spend it in your office or on the roads, or in the court-house answering stupid questions from a clever lawyer does not affect your salary. As for the humiliation, well, I fear there's nothing in Civil Service Procedure that refers to compensation for such. In any case why are you here today, Mr Oti?'

'It is this letter, from the D.O.' He handed the letter to him.

'Oh yes,' McBain said, glancing through the letter. 'Inviting you to appear before the Commission of Inquiry investigating the charges of irregularities against your Foreman. I know all about it, Mr Oti.'

'But I do not intend to appear before that Commission or any other Commission of Inquiry in connection with anything to do with the Foreman.'

'Oh, just why, Mr Oti, may I ask?' he said, in a rather tired voice.

'Because I'm thoroughly fed up with the case and with Mr Simeon Oke. I feel I've suffered sufficient humiliation in the court. And I do not intend to be subjected to further humiliation at a Commission of Inquiry. The fellow has been discharged in a court of law. Discharged and acquitted. I do not now see why we are bothering ourselves about him any more.'

'Civil Service regulations and procedure, Mr Oti. The courts have tried him on the charges of stealing and conspiracy to defraud Government. The penalty is a long-term imprisonment and/or the payment of a heavy fine – could be both. He has been found not guilty and discharged and acquitted by the magistrate. You and I are engineers, Mr Oti. We do not belong to the learned profession and so cannot appreciate the depth of the learning which led the magistrate to his learned judgement. Perhaps to do even that would amount to contempt of court. It is a serious matter, Mr Oti,' he said as Titus smiled at the obviously ridiculous state of affairs.

'Meanwhile, the discharge and acquittal of Simeon Oke does not in any way prove that he is exactly an angel. Has he, in fact, behaved in the best tradition of a civil servant in His Majesty's Colonial Service? Is he fit to continue as an employee of the Nigerian Government? There are certain regulations laid down in the Civil Service Code for looking into these matters. Your Commission of Inquiry has been set up in accordance with these regulations. I fear you cannot escape it, Mr Oti. Civil Service procedure, you see.'

Titus was the first witness before Prosser, the Sole Commissioner. The Commissioner tried to put him at ease by apologizing for taking him away from his very onerous duties to come and give evidence at the Inquiry. He realized how much of his time had already been wasted in the case that had already been decided in the Magistrate's Court. As much as possible he would see to it that his evidence did not take a long time.

After a few routine questions the Commissioner asked: 'As District Engineer you are responsible for the activities of Simeon Oke, the Foreman?'

'For his activities, whenever such activities are official, and lawful,' Titus answered guardedly.

'And, Mr Oti, it is your responsibility to check from time to time that papers sent up to you for approval by the Foreman are in order.'

'Yes, that is correct.'

'Would you say that Simeon Oke has always been honest in the papers he has put up to you for approval?'

'I honestly cannot say.'

164

'You honestly cannot say. Take the case of the mileage allowance claims that he has made in respect of his car, No. CL 457. Would you say that those claims have always been true?'

'I took his certificate on the voucher as sufficient reason to trust him,' Titus said. He had to admit to himself that he knew very well that, certificate or no certificate, he did not trust the Foreman.

'But are you yourself not obliged to see that, in spite of the Foreman's certificate, he actually does the mileage in respect of which he makes a claim for payment?'

Titus frowned. Prosser was going to behave to type. 'I'm only obliged to see that the journeys done were necessary and to certify to that effect. Honestly, I do not see how I could be expected to follow him round every mile of road in Ibala District.'

'Of course you're right, Mr Oti. No one expects you to follow him round every mile of road. The trouble is, you see, Simeon Oke's car was alleged to have been rotting away at the All Races Club for weeks together. You have not seen it there yourself, Mr Oti?'

Titus had a silent battle with himself as he recalled the incident of his meeting Bimpe at the All Races and having the car pointed out to him. 'I believe the Police investigated this matter, sir. I understand they found nothing to substantiate the allegation.'

The Commissioner made some notes. His clerk made his notes rather importantly. The police orderly in attendance removed his fez, wiped with the back of his left hand the beads of perspiration from his shining forehead and later screwed the cap back on his head. Titus relaxed in the witness stand.

'Now, Mr Oti, you have no doubt heard that some of your road labourers were caught working on a private farm near Iwana on 21 May last?'

'Yes, I have heard so.'

'Do you know if the farm in question belongs to Simeon Oke the Foreman?'

'No, I do not know.'

'Do you know that the road labourers were working on the farm at all?'

'No, not till I got the information after the Police raid. If I knew P.W.D. employees were working on a private farm I would myself have reported the matter to the Police.'

'Of course you would, like a responsible Senior Government Official,' Prosser said in a way that left Titus guessing as to whether this was meant to be a compliment or not.

The third witness was one of the two labourers alleged to have been caught working on Simeon's private farm. He had already gone through the ordeal of the court case, first as an accused and later as crown witness. He was already getting used to the drill.

'You did work on the farm near Iwana, Dada?'

'Yes, I did. We all worked on the farm.'

The Commissioner frowned. 'I want you to confine your evidence to your own part,' he said to the witness via the interpreter. 'Let others say their parts. For how long did you work on the farm?'

'I worked there for seven weeks. *Oga* told me to work there. He told all of us to work there. And—'

'You worked there for seven weeks,' the Commissioner wrote down something. 'And your *Oga* told you to work on the farm. Did *Oga* Simeon the Foreman tell you himself to work on the farm?'

'No. He sent the headman to us.'

'So it was the headman and not the Foreman who instructed you to go to the farm?'

'Yes, it was the headman.'

166

'But how do you know that the headman was telling the truth? The Foreman might not have instructed him to instruct you to go to the farm. Do you not think so?'

'I do not know.'

'You do not know,' he said, making a note of it on his pad. The Clerk of the Commission wrote importantly at his desk. 'Now, Dada, when you were working on the farm did you think that you were working for Government?'

'I thought I was working for Government.'

'You thought then that the farm belonged to Government and not to the Foreman?'

'I thought that the farm belonged to Government.'

'You did not know that the farm belonged to the Foreman?'

'No. I did not.'

The next witness was the timekeeper in the office of the District Engineer of Ibala.

'As timekeeper, is it your duty to mark in your book the people who are present as well as those who are absent?'

'No. That is not correct,' the man answered very guardedly. He was a fat man. He sweated profusely.

'Is it not correct that you mark present people that are present?' the Commissioner asked in a mixture of surprise and irritation.

'I mark present only people that are present. I do not mark present people that are not present. To do that would be against the regulations. I do not do anything against the regulations.'

'You must answer my questions concisely, and don't ramble all over the place. You mark present only those that are present?'

'That is correct, sir.'

'And you mark absent all those that are absent?'

'Yes. I mark absent all those that are absent.'

'And do you yourself see the men before you mark them present? Or do you rely on what the Foreman or the headman tells you?'

'It is my duty to see the men before marking them present. That is the regulation,' the fat man said, wiping beads of perspiration off his face. The Commission Clerk wrote furiously at his desk.

'I want you to tell me what you do, not what you should do according to the regulation.'

'According to the regulation, I must see the men before marking them present. And I must not go against the regulation.'

The Commissioner tightened his lips in suppressed anger at the witness who, he thought, was hedging. Then he said 'Will you now answer this question with a "yes" or a "no". Do you know Dada?'

'I do not know which Dada you mean.'

The Commissioner ordered that the last witness be brought back. 'This is Dada. Do you know him?'

'Yes, I know him.'

'Is he one of the employees of your Department.'

'Yes, he is one of the workers on the Ibala–Iwana Road.'

'On 21 May last did you see him working on the road?'

'I do not remember.'

'Did you mark him present or absent in your book that day?'

'I do not remember.'

'If you marked him present, would that mean that you saw him working on the Ibala-Iwana Road that day?'

'Yes, it would mean that I saw him working on the road.'

'On that particular day the Police raided a farm on the Ibala–Iwana Road. And Dada was found working on that farm. Therefore you ought not to have marked him present on that day.'

The timekeeper looked thoughtful for some time. He looked worried. Then he said 'Master, this my work is hard. I pray to God every day that He may help me, for my work is hard.'

The Commissioner regarded him with interest, sucking tenderly at the stem of his pipe. He nodded his head in encouragement to the witness to go on.

'You see, Master, when I go round the road in the morning, I see the men working on the road. So I mark them present in my book. That is according to regulations. When I go round in the afternoon, I see the men still working on the roads. So I complete the marking in my book. Master, that is the truth. And I've done this for thirteen years.'

The Clerk of the Commission wrote fast.

'Master, I beg you, I have no hand in this matter,' the timekeeper pleaded, and he went flat on his tummy to beg the Commissioner to let him go.

'You mark the workers present in your book when you see them both in the morning and in the afternoon ... Yes? Between those two points of time how can you tell that they are working on the road?'

'Master, I cannot tell,' the timekeeper said. 'Master, I am a Roman Catholic. I do not tell lies—'

'Of course you cannot tell,' the Commissioner said, cutting short his religious details. He made copious notes.

Twenty-four

———————◇———————

HE wrote to his dear Bola just before going to bed one Saturday night. 'Mother has again been here today. I avoided another row with her. To tell the truth I had neither the strength nor the desire for another row. So when she came just after supper, and as usual unannounced, I did not question her. And when she opened the infernal subject of the relations between me and Simeon, between me and Pastor Morakinyo, and between me and Pa Joel, I listened to her but said nothing. But, Bola, I tell you it was hell listening to her illogical, sentimental arguments and pleadings.

'Her main argument was that the judge knew everything and if it was true that Simeon committed the crime, he would have known and so sent him to prison. Pastor Morakinyo has said that Simeon did not commit the crime and so she believed him as she and the whole lot of them take everything that Pastor Morakinyo says as gospel truth. Did I not see how everyone was happy after the judge had discharged and acquitted him? Did I not see them all, the road overseers and the sectionmen and the contractors, all shouting for joy? Did I not see the members of the church in the courthouse singing Allelujah? Did I not see the way Simeon was carried shoulder-high out of the courthouse? These were the questions she asked me.

'I was tempted to ask her if she knew that the labourers who came to give evidence for the prosecution had been frightened and confused by the Police, and that those who came to give evidence for the defence had been bribed by Simeon and his well-wishers. I was tempted to ask her if she knew that Pa Joel's evidence was influenced by his great fear of Oluode the family god to speak the truth as to whether or not he had given the piece of farm land to Simeon. Bola, how the old man is scared of Oluode and Ajobi! Like all of them, his Christianity is only skin-deep. He believes more in his Oluode who he thinks can cause him a violent death than in the God he goes to worship at church twice every Sunday. Pastor Morakinyo's fault, to my mind. He has painted the Christian God as a forgiving father, slow to chide and swift to bless.

'But why should I bore you with these details, when indeed I should be telling you how much I love you and how I am looking forward with mounting excitement to the day when you will come back? Won't that be heavenly, darling? But you know that if I had no understanding person like you to whom I could state my own side of this case in which everyone here says I am wrong and Simeon my corrupt kinsman is right I am sure I would go mad, stark-staring mad. I'm sure you would rather listen to my tale of woes now than return in another four months to a raving lunatic.

'Talking about your coming back in four months reminds me of the happenings here centred round one of my road section-men called Bandele. He was the man who saw the vision of the world coming to an end at Pa Matthew's – you remember I mentioned the fantastic incident in one of my letters. Well, Bandele has alleged that he has had two more visions since then, all to the effect that the end of the world was truly coming. He has now, in fact, fixed a date for Judgement Day! 12 August which is just under a month from now! You won't believe how Bandele has suddenly become important, how large crowds go to Elder Matthew's house at dawn and at night where Matthew assisted by Bandele and a whole band of prophets and prophetesses, are preparing the crowds against the coming of the Lord!

'Yes, you can laugh as much as you like, girl. Of course it must be nonsense. But supposing it is NOT nonsense – supposing the end of the world does come in another three and a half weeks, which is before you come back and before we get married. Then what becomes of us? Have you thought of all this? Nonsense, of course. But remember that it is written in the Scriptures that the Last Day will come and catch people completely unprepared. So, my girl, you had better give more thought to your religious exercises that your own devotion may save both you and sinful me from the wrath to come.

'One of the things Mother came to tell me is that I must go to church tomorrow. It is a special thanksgiving service, first and foremost for the discharge and acquittal of Simeon, and secondly for the restoration of peace in the family, particularly between Simeon and me! Everybody is looking forward to my attending the service. And I've decided to attend.'

Pastor Morakinyo was in excellent form at the thanksgiving service the following morning. 'It is all the work of the Devil,' he thundered from the pulpit. 'At the bottom of all our troubles both as individuals, as members of this church and as co-workers in Government work – at the bottom of them all is the Evil One, the sower of evil seeds on fertile soil, the sower of discord between friends, between relations, and among peaceful communities.

'We who are, by training and experience, familiar with the usual tactics of the Evil One have known for some time that he had been feeling for weak points in our defences from which to launch his sinister offensive. First he originated the rumour that the very strong pillar of our church was to be knocked off from under us. For how else can anyone interpret the rumoured transfer of our well-beloved Brother Simeon to a strange country called the Cameroons? I ask you, my brethren in Christ, could our church have recovered from the blow if Brother Simeon had been transferred away from us?'

They all groaned, and nodded their heads in agreement with him that All Souls could not have sustained for a month the absence of Simeon from Ibala.

'Having originated the rumour which he spread both among our members and the rest of the community, Satan then planted in the hearts of all people that our well-respected Engineer Titus was responsible for the transfer.'

Again groans and nods indicated that the congregation were with the preacher in his brilliant analysis of the Devil's activities.

'Look at him, look at our Engineer Titus, the brightest gem in the crown of our church of All Souls and of our town Ibala. Who here did not know him as a most saintly boy with the heart of a cherub? Yet for the purpose of carrying out his diabolical plans the Evil One made people believe that it was he who was at the bottom of the transfer of his kinsman the Foreman. I ask you in all seriousness: would Titus Oti that we all know do a thing like this? No, I agree with you. He would not; he did not. But the Devil made most people believe that he did. He made Simeon believe that his kinsman did and for a brief moment the Devil nearly succeeded in his plans. Nearly, but not quite, thanks be to God.

'But the Destroyer did not stop there. He made Engineer Titus believe for a brief moment that his kinsman the Foreman was not a good man at his work.' There were groans from the congregation at the absurdity of the thing. The pastor then traced the career of Simeon in the P.W.D. and showed how it would not make sense for anyone to think that he could have had such a distinguished career if he had not been good at his work. 'But it was the Evil One and not Titus, our Titus, that levied the accusation of inefficiency, of corruption – yes corruption – and dishonesty – against our dear Brother Simeon.'

He wiped his brow, and allowed the groaning of the congregation to subside before proceeding: 'And look at Sister Deborah, a veritable mother in Israel, the saintly soul that had in all these trying times been making strenuous efforts to bring peace between her son and his kinsman the Foreman. Look at her.' He himself set the example by staring at Deborah who sat in the third pew. Titus, too, looked at his mother from where he sat at the other end of the pew. He thought that she took the stare of the congregation rather well. 'Who in this congregation did not know how very much this Christian woman has performed her duties to her husband of blessed memory, to her son Engineer Titus, and to her benefactor Brother Simeon? Who here does not know how she has publicly expressed her indebtedness to Brother Simeon Oke since her dear husband died? And yet the Evil One succeeded for a brief moment in making this same woman accuse her great benefactor of attempting to murder Engineer Titus, her son.' They all groaned at the absurdity.

After going on in this strain for some time he wound

174

up: 'We mortals sometimes wonder why our Father in Heaven exposes us His children to the machinations of the Evil One. We sometimes wonder why He does not destroy the Destroyer once and for all instead of allowing him to sow the seeds of dissension between friend and friend, between mother and son, between kinsman and kinsman. It is the usual method our Lord employs to train His chosen to stand up to the wiles and guiles of the Devil. In the end He stretches out His saving hand first to save His own and then to crush the Devil. We rejoice that the Lord of All Souls has stretched out His saving hand to the family of our dearly respected Elder Joel to save them all – Sister Deborah, Brother Simeon, Engineer Titus and Elder Joel himself from the wickedness of the Devil. We rejoice as a church that Brother Simeon is now completely restored to us, unblemished, ready once more to take his place at the head of the army of the builders of our church. We must all pray as a church that the peace that has now returned to the family of Elder Joel and to the church of All Souls may be lasting peace.'

After the service the whole congregation were entertained lavishly in the house of Pa Joel. It was practically a repeat of the festivities that took place after the thanksgiving service held the first Sunday after Titus arrived back from England.

Twenty-five

———————◇———————

AUGUST 12, the day Judgement Day came to Ibala, started like any other day. The cock crowed at dawn as usual. The men and women, as usual, rose as the cock crew, but only a few men went to the farms, and only a few of the women went to the brooks and to the markets. A majority decided to stay indoors and meet Judgement Day within the safety of their own hearths.

But the *Alasoteles* or the band of the faithful, as the prophets and prophetesses of Ibala had come to be known, had resolved not to be caught unawares by the ordinariness of the day which they were certain was going to be the Last. Some of them had already started their religious exercises in their individual homes reading psalms and singing from the hymn-book. Others had decided that the wisest thing to do was to make straight for Elder Matthew's. The crowd at the usual house of prayer therefore grew fast, quite early in the day. Enough prophets and prophetesses had assembled long before noon to give leadership to the psalm-reading and the hymn-singing and the clapping of hands. And, by noon, the usual meeting-place in the backyard was already full and had overflown through the central corridor of Elder Matthew's house on to the front verandah and thence to the road outside – the main trunk road from Ibadan through Ibala to Northern Nigeria.

By noon too the clouds had gathered and the sky was already overcast. It was obvious there was going to be a storm. This was, of course, not unusual in ordinary circumstances on an August day. But the circumstances were not ordinary and ordinary events were regarded with ominous significance.

For Titus the day started badly. At the bridge construction site at the Iwana Gate there were only three men when he called at about 10 a.m. These scrambled to their feet when they saw him. He wanted to know where the others were; there should have been thirteen others, two carpenters, four bricklayers and seven labourers. The three men replied that they did not know where their comrades were.

'And why are you not working instead of just sitting down?' he fumed at them.

'D.E., the headman is not here. He has the key to the store.' He drove away furiously. If the threatening storm should come that day it would almost certainly cause a flood that would wash away the temporary diversion at the bridge site.

Back in the office he noticed that his Chief Clerk, his accounts clerk and his engineering assistant, together with a large number of others, were absent. The droning of the planing machine in the distance indicated that a few people had turned up for work in the workshops.

The messenger came in through the door and gave the salute. He told him that all the Christians in town had been ordered to assemble and had gone to the house of Elder Matthew. All the Moslems in town had been similarly ordered to assemble at the central mosque. He said the Chief Clerk, the account's clerk, the timekeeper and all the others had gone. He was waiting to tell the D.E. of this important thing and to warn him to go to Elder Matthew's as he knew he was a good Christian. He also waited to have D.E.'s official permission before going off to the Mosque.

Titus listened with interest to the messenger. He noticed that he had arranged, as he always did, the incoming-mail in a pile apart from the other papers.

'Do you really want to go to the Mosque, Musa?' he asked, as he lifted a fat envelope marked O.H.M.S. 'You are a Moslem. Surely the Imam hasn't told you the world is coming to an end today? Only the world of the *Alasoteles* believe it, not so?'

'May Allah prolong your life, Master. The *Alasoteles* are Christians. We are Moslems. But Moslems and Christians are brothers, Master.'

Titus waved Musa away as he settled down to read the contents of the envelope. First, a forwarding letter from the Provincial Engineer, McBain. Then five sheets of a report signed by Prosser. He read the sheets with interest, frowns and smiles marking the progress of what he read and his reaction to it. He read the concluding paragraphs twice.

'I fear the evidence against Simeon Oke in connection with the two P.W.D. men working on the farm near Iwana is most slim. I must say, however, that I do not accept the evidence of Joel Tobatele the old head of the family that he did not give the farmland to Simeon Oke as sufficient reason to conclude that Simeon Oke was not in *de facto* if not in *de jure* possession of the farm. Tribal customs are breaking down fast and it is not inconceivable that the influential and wealthy Simeon Oke might have taken possession of a piece of family farmland without seeking and obtaining the approval of the head of the family. In spite of this I am unable to say categorically that the farm is Simeon Oke's and I reluctantly give him the benefit of the doubt.

'If there is doubt about the guilt of Simeon Oke there is no doubt whatsoever in my mind that the road section-man in charge of the men caught working on the farm is guilty of a criminal offence. I understand this man is not yet on the permanent establishment and I recommend that his appointment should be terminated forthwith. I recommend this instead of criminal proceedings as these will be tedious and long, and the results will not be worth the effort. The two labourers concerned are also daily paid staff and they too should have their appointment terminated as well.

'Again I have no direct evidence of fraud against Simeon Oke in respect of motor-car mileage claims. There was no evidence whatsoever forthcoming about car No. CL 457 lying idle for days in the premises of the All Races Club. I am unable to convince myself, however, that all the journeys recorded were necessary and econo-mical. These journeys were, however, certified, author-ized and done in the interest of Government by the local head of department.

'From all the foregoing I come to the conclusion that enough evidence has not been forthcoming to warrant the dismissal of Simeon Oke from Government Service under Sections 48 and 49 of the Civil Service Code. I am, however, convinced that it is not in the interest of Government that he should continue to work in Ibala. I recommend therefore that he should be transferred away from Ibala to another place where he will make a new beginning.

'At the risk of exceeding my terms of reference I observe that this Inquiry has yielded sufficient revela-tions to make the authorities of the Department of Public Works consider a complete reorganization of that department, particularly at the district level. The District Engineer Ibala is very hardworking and, I am glad to say, his integrity is beyond reproach. But he will be the first to admit that there are lots of loose ends that need tightening in Ibala. It is because of such loose ends that Simeon Oke and his associates have been able to carry out their activities which, even though not proved criminal, are certainly not in the best interest of Government. I have had the opportunity of discussing this with the Provincial Engineer in Ibadan and I am happy to record that he assures me that his department are already considering the type of reorganization I have in mind.'

Titus was annoyed. Again Simeon Oke had escaped. He had himself anticipated this when he heard that a Commission of Inquiry was to be set up. He had expressed the view in one of his letters that it was just impossible to catch Simeon or anyone else in the circumstances where everyone appeared to be the friend of the guilty and the criminal and no one was prepared to run the risk of unpopularity by coming forward to aid the law.

He was annoyed that Prosser had used the Inquiry to make disparaging remarks about his administration of Ibala District. He thought this was all part of his prejudice against him as an African heading a district.

Looking through the window he saw Chris Daniels's Pontiac sweep into the yard. Bimpe was with him.

'Ah, Titus Oti, Auntie Bimp here wants me to tell you that you are the first person she's seen today,' Chris was saying as both he and Bimpe came along the corridor towards the District Engineer's office. 'You no doubt know the significance of this.'

'Lawyer, I've told you this is not just any day,' Bimpe said as she led her companion into the room. 'Good morning, D.E.'

'Good morning, Auntie Bimp. I trust you are well,' Titus said, inhaling her perfume. She was, as usual, very neatly dressed in her combination of brown and cream. Her shoes were white. But she had no trinkets on, except for a pair of gold ear-rings.

'Auntie Bimp has come in to say good morning, and from what I see, good-bye to you, Titus, till you both meet again in Kingdom Come, which I gather is round the corner.'

'Lawyer, this is no joking matter.'

'You, Titus boy, have lived the life of a saint, honest and incorruptible and all that. All evidence is that at least you should qualify to go to Heaven. But as for me—'

'D.E., I don't want you to listen to Lawyer. He takes everything as a joke,' Bimpe said, taking a cigarette from Titus's pack. 'I want us to go to Pa Matthew's place now. There is a special prayer meeting going on there now.'

'During office hours – that's impossible, Auntie Bimp.'

'You're the head of your department here; who's going to query you about what you do? Besides, is it a bad thing to be caught praying?'

'Particularly on the Last Day,' Chris commented, puffing out a sophisticated ring of smoke.

'But, Auntie Bimp, do you too believe seriously in this Last Day stuff?' Titus asked, regarding her with pity.

'Look, D.E., I want you to come with me now. I beg you, D.E.,' she pleaded.

'Oh, Auntie Bimp, I really cannot.'

'D.E., is this all I mean to you?' she asked, bewitchingly.

'You mean everything in the world to him,' Chris assured her. 'Everything in the world. The man is only an engineer. Men of that profession have difficulty in professing their love.'

Then Bimpe regarded both of them strangely. She looked from one to the other. She got up and said, 'Lawyer, I want your driver to take me to Pa Matthew's now. Right now. D.E.,' she said from the corridor, 'I want you to follow. Don't be late.'

'She's made the best decision, Titus,' Chris said as he watched his Pontiac drive out of the yard. 'There's something in the Holy Book about everyone fighting out his own salvation on the Day of Judgement. Some warning to the effect that husband should not wait for wife, and father not wait for son.'

'He at the roof-top not to come down for the purpose of taking something from inside the house, or something to that effect,' Titus joined in the fun. 'I say, Chris, it has truly been said that the Devil himself will quote the scripture for his diabolical plans.'

'Titus, I think you have another messenger, bidding you come to Pa Matthew's. Your last chance, this time.'

'Pastor Morakinyo,' Titus observed looking through the window. 'No, he's an Anglican divine. He hates the *Alasoteles* like the plague. He's certainly not coming to talk about the Last Day.

'About Kingdom Come in some other form, I shall bet you. Titus, I don't trust these men who wear their white collar the other way round.'

Twenty-six

───────◇───────

'COME right in, sir,' Titus said as he noticed that Pastor Morakinyo hesitated at the door. 'Good morning, sir.'

'Good morning, Engineer, I'm sorry I didn't tell you I was coming,' he apologized, shaking hands with Titus.

'That's perfectly all right, sir. You remember Mr Daniels, sir?'

'Remember Mr Daniels?' Pastor Morakinyo repeated. 'Can I ever forget Mr Daniels? Can our entire congregation of All Souls ever forget the man who saved Brother Simeon?' He shook hands with Chris enthusiastically.

Titus offered him a more comfortable chair than the stool on which he first perched diffidently, placing his black hat on his lap. Titus took the hat from him and hung it on a peg. 'I'm sorry my messenger isn't here, sir, to attend to you. All of them, including my Chief Clerk, are gone. Something to do with today being the Day of Judgement,' Titus said, looking at his visitor whilst Chris grinned.

'Engineer Titus, I must confess I'm myself worried about the whole thing,' Morakinyo said. 'It is a good thing to be at all times ready for the second coming of Our Lord. It is true we are taught in the Scriptures to expect it to be sudden. But the way the *Alasoteles* have worked up the people into this frenzy is most strange.'

'Today, then, is not the Last Day, sir?' Chris asked feigning seriousness. Titus frowned. He disapproved of his taking the simple cleric for a ride in his office.

'Of course not, sir,' Morakinyo said. 'Of course not.'

After an embarrassing silence Chris indicated that he wanted to leave. He guessed the clergyman would want to be alone with Titus. But it was Morakinyo himself who stopped him from leaving. 'What I've come for, Engineer Titus, is Brother Simeon,' he said. 'Barrister Daniels is one of us, after his brilliant defence of Brother Simeon. I think he should stay to advise us, Engineer.'

'What's the trouble now?' Titus asked.

'Transfer. They again want to transfer him, Engineer.'

'They want to transfer him,' Titus repeated, wondering that Pastor Morakinyo was already in possession of the recommendations of the Prosser Report. He groaned inwardly at the fear that the contents of the Report, supposed to be so secret that it had been put in two envelopes, one sealed inside the other, had in fact become common property no doubt via the confidential clerk and the typist and the messenger first in Prosser's office and next in McBain's. As he was wondering what to tell the vicar the telephone rang.

'Yes, good morning, Mr Prosser,' he said into the receiver.

'Thank God, at least you are at work,' the voice at the other end cried. 'Whatever is all this madness going on in town?'

Titus did not answer. Prosser went on regardless: 'I hear some bloke has read his Bible upside-down and identified today as the Day of Judgement. I hear the central figure is one of your road section-men, some crank called Bandele.'

'Oh yes,' Titus said, for politeness.

'Precious value the tax-payers are getting for their money, what with dishonest foremen and prophesying section-men. But look, Mr Oti, I don't care myself whether the heavens fall today or tomorrow or the day after, what I want is someone to do something about the traffic jam.'

'Traffic jam; where, Mr Prosser?'

'Yes, traffic jam; at Iwana Road. The whole place is jammed solid. This is normally a matter for the Police – and I've phoned the Superintendent of Police. But I think, apart from the crowd of people waiting to see Jesus coming through the clouds descending, one of the main causes of the traffic jam is one of your P.W.D. lorries parked on the wrong side of the road. I gather your Foreman is there. Kindly do something about it, Mr Oti.'

A few minutes after all three of them, Titus, Chris Daniels and Pastor Morakinyo were on their way to the Iwana Road. Titus had explained to his companions what the District Officer had told him and the necessity for him to do something about the traffic jam. Pastor Morakinyo would have gone ahead on his old bicycle had they not discovered that the front tyre had gone flat. In the circumstances Titus had offered the vicar a ride in the lawyer's car – he would arrange for someone to mend the flat tyre and send the bicycle to the vicarage later on.

The car came upon the crowd quite suddenly, after sweeping out of Hospital Road, on which the P.W.D. yard was situated, and entering the main road which was part of the trunk road through the town. In his report on the episode of 12 August 1950, in Ibala, Titus later emphasized that the episode would not have been complicated by the traffic jam and accidents had the trunk road not passed through the town. He took the opportunity to press once more for the construction of a ring road on to which all through traffic would be diverted.

A police constable came running to the car in difficulty, saluted smartly – all police constables knew the lawyer's car and the lawyer's importance. He gave a second salute, this time after he had discovered that the District Engineer and Pastor Morakinyo were in the car. He explained to them that it was impossible to go any farther in the car and advised them to proceed on foot.

'Where's the Police Superintendent, Constable?' Titus asked, as he came out of the car.

'Somewhere in the crowd, sir. I don't know exactly where, D.E. The crowd is so thick.'

'So I see, Constable. You are supposed to be clearing the traffic jam. I don't see you achieving much success.'

'But, D.E., it is impossible. No one can do anything about this traffic today,' the police constable explained. 'Whenever anyone arrived, he got out of his car, and joined the crowd. No one bothers to listen to the Police.'

Chris was the first to notice that Pastor Morakinyo was no longer with them and called the attention of Titus to the missing parson. Titus said he thought they must have lost him as they inched their way through the crowd towards Pa Matthew's house, which they imagined was the centre of activities.

'The old boy, I think, has effected his escape,' Chris commented. 'Quite understandable, he cannot stand the indignity of playing the part of an ordinary onlooker at this most important function where one of his own church elders is the officiating priest assisted by a road section-man.'

Titus laughed.

'No laughing matter, this,' Chris continued rather seriously. 'Can you think of any event more important in the Church's two thousand years' history than this, the second coming of Jesus Christ, via the clouds over Ibala.'

Titus chuckled again. They both continued, making painfully slow progress through the crowd. 'An outlandish place to choose for such a holy event,' Chris said philosophically. 'No doubt in the tradition of the First Coming through the insignificant village of Bethlehem. Still.'

Titus paused. It was necessary to take bearings. It was impossible to do anything about traffic control that day. Except by the luckiest chance, he was certain he couldn't find the Police Superintendent in that crowd. He was certain that even if he found him he wouldn't be able to do a thing about the traffic either.

All around him, Titus noticed that men and women sang songs of praise. Some recited psalms. There was no identifiable leadership. There were pockets at the centre of which a particular activity like singing or psalm-reciting or praying prevailed with a number of other minor but allied activities on the fringes. Just then Titus and Chris found themselves in a solid pocket of strenuous hymn-singing.

Titus dragged Chris on towards another section of the crowd, where the main activity seemed to be preaching. When they had got near enough to hear the main speaker distinctly they stopped.

'Ah, this then is THE Day, brethren,' the speaker said. Titus noticed that he wore a white shirt, a pair of khaki shorts, a pair of canvas slippers, and carried a bell in his hand.

'This must be your road section-man, Titus. We had better keep close to him, that he may put in a word for you, and for me your friend.'

'Hear what he's saying,' Titus said seriously. 'This is not a section-man – this is not Bandele. The way he speaks shows he's either a trained preacher or—'

'He's inspired by the Holy Spirit, man.'

'I congratulate you all on your singularly good fortune,' the speaker continued. 'You and I cannot appreciate the full significance of this day. This is the day in respect of which countless generations of the faithful in all lands have been praying: Thy Kingdom Come, Thy Kingdom Come. Countless are the millions who have lived lives of holiness and faith and would have given anything to have lived to see this day. But it was destined that they should first submit to the powers of death before rising again today. Allelujah—'

'Allelujah!' the crowd shouted after him.

'It has been given to you and me, miserable sinners, the joy of seeing this most memorable day without first being overcome by the powers of death. But unfortunately there are millions whom this day has caught unprepared to welcome the Bridegroom – dining and drinking and committing sins and indulging in worldly desires.

'We are grateful to Father who has given us grace to be caught prepared. We shall pray to God to forgive us our trespasses. We shall pray God to forgive those millions who have failed to heed the warning that the coming of the Bridegroom would be unannounced. We must make special supplications to God Almighty that our sins and transgressions may be washed away in the last few moments of this world of sin and woe. Allelu—'

'Allelujah!'

'Allelu—'

'Allelujah!'

'Allelu—'

'Allelujah!'

Down went that part of the crowd in the immediate vicinity of the speaker with the bell, regardless of the hard tarmac and the laterite which bit into and coloured their knees. Titus noticed what he had seen on an earlier occasion that some shouted their prayers at the top of their voices, completely ignoring the presence of neighbours. Others said their prayers in whispers. One woman merely cried, 'Father, Father, Father, Amen; Father, Father, Father, Amen!' over and over again.

'Titus, d'you hear that?' Chris asked. 'Sounds like a woman in distress. Let's move nearer.'

Twenty-seven

---◇---

'FATHER,' the woman in distress was crying. 'Father, I paid only 5s 6d for the head-scarf which I bought for the sister of my husband at Oshogbo last month which I told her I bought for 7s. I ask for forgiveness, Father. I promise to pay to my sister-in-law the 1s 6d of which I cheated her.'

'Allelu—' one of the leaders cried.

'Allelujah!' the crowd thundered in reply.

'I forgive my brother's wife from the bottom of my heart,' another woman cried from the crowd. 'The head-scarf was a good bargain for 7s and she need not refund any money to me. I confess here to having nursed a grievance against my brother's wife for over nine years. I ask her for her forgiveness. I ask Father to wash away my sins today.'

'Allelu—'

'Allelujah!'

Then another woman cried, 'I did something terrible to my husband's third wife, and I now ask for forgiveness. It was I who beat her goat and broke its leg after it had eaten my yams in the kitchen. I ask for her forgiveness and for God's forgiveness for having lied to her and to all at home that some rascally schoolboy must have been responsible for maiming the goat.'

'Allelu—'

'Allelujah!'

Then a man spoke: 'I am a great sinner,' he confessed. 'When I had been ill for several weeks together some time last year and there was no sign of improvement even though I prayed regularly and drank holy water and bathed the affected area with holy water, I allowed one of my wives to persuade me to take a native doctor's medicine. I ask for forgiveness and promise never again to let my faith flag.'

'Allelu—'

'Allelujah!'

'Good Lord,' Chris whispered. 'Is it an offence to take medicine when one is ill? Why, then, the doctors should all pack up and the hospitals be converted into schools.'

'No, not schools,' Titus had caught something of the hysteria of the moment. 'They should be converted into houses of prayer. Good God, listen to that, Auntie Bimp's voice, I'm certain,' he said excitedly.

'I am a very sinful woman,' Bimpe said. 'I have always been jealous of my younger sister. She's more fortunate than I am in many ways. And there are many other things for which I need God's forgiveness.'

'Allelu—'

'Allelujah!'

'My word, Titus, that was a very close shave,' Chris said sweating. 'I was afraid she was going to say some rather embarrassing things. I suggest we leave – at once.'

Titus agreed and they tried to but it was impossible.

Yet another woman sobbed out her confession. 'I dare not look my husband in the face any more,' she said. 'I have been standing up to the Devil's temptation for a long time, but I fell only last week. It was the brother

of my husband that made me unfaithful to my husband.
I ask for, for—' and the woman broke down, in tears.

'Ah, Alice!' a man cried out in the crowd.

'Say you forgive Alice, Brother,' one of the prophets
ordered.

'Ah, Alice,' the Brother repeated in distress.

'Your husband has forgiven you, Sister,' the prophet
said. 'And God has forgiven you both, Allelu—'

'Allelujah!'

'Ah, Titus, your Foreman, if I'm not mistaken,' Chris
said, pointing to Simeon. He was only a few yards
away.

'My kinsman, my esteemed Foreman to be sure,' Titus
said. 'I know he is one of the leaders of this movement.'

'I say, Titus, watch him,' Chris shouted as they both
saw Simeon make movements which indicated that he
was labouring under some great mental strain. First,
still kneeling, he cried, 'Father, Father, Father.' Then,
with difficulty he rose to his feet, rolled his eyes heaven-
wards, and then dropped back on his knees again crying
'Father, Father!!'

Chris heaved a loud sigh of relief but Titus was
disappointed. They both thought the seizure was over.

But it was not, for Simeon Oke again cried: 'Father
of all Mercies, I am a miserable sinner. I ask God Almighty
to forgive me my sins. . . . I took money from the
carpenters and masons that I engaged to work in the
P.W.D. before I employed them. They themselves
offered me the money, and I did not force anyone to
give me money. I ask for God's forgiveness for the
bribes that I took. I shall pay back the people concerned—'

'I forgive the Foreman in respect of the 25s he took
from me,' one man cried. He was only a yard or two
from Titus and Chris. 'I ask God's forgiveness for having

reported the matter to a Police friend of mine. I know, however, that the policeman did not do anything about it.'

'Allelu—'

'Allelujah!'

But Simeon Oke continued, 'For many months I claimed more mileage allowances in respect of my car than I was entitled to. I was tempted by the Devil to do this because my salary was not enough to support me and my family. I also wanted money to contribute towards the building of our new church. I ask God's forgiveness for all that I have done wrong.'

'Allelu—'

'Allelujah.'

'And I ask for God's forgiveness for many more things that I have done wrong,' Simeon said, to Titus's extreme disappointment. He wished the old crook would not lump together the rest of his sins in a sort of package deal. But the next minute Simeon particularized. 'In particular I ask for forgiveness for the lies I told in the court about the P.W.D. labourers who were found working on the farm near Iwana. I instructed the section-man to take the labourers there. . . . The farm was mine. I am sorry to have lied in court that the farm was not mine. I ask for God's forgiveness for all my sins.'

Twenty-eight

———————◇———————

'My brethren in Christ, the more we mortals try to know
the whys and wherefores of the ways of the Lord our
God the more we find ourselves hopelessly in difficulty.'
Rev. Morakinyo was addressing his congregation from
the pulpit of All Souls at a Sunday morning service
seven weeks after the events of 12 August 1950, at
Ibala.

'We sometimes wonder why the Lord, the good Lord,
allows the only son of a good Christian couple to die
while he allows the family of the unjust and the wicked
to flourish and to prosper. We sometimes wonder why
the Lord, the good Lord, allows his rain of blessing to
fall on the farm of the just as well as on the farm of the
unjust. Why was it that the Lord our God allowed Job
to suffer all the dreadful things he suffered? The more
we try to unfathom these mysteries the more we find
that it is nothing but our faith in the goodness of the
Lord our God that prevents our Christian belief from
turning into unbelief. We must be happy, however, that
from time to time God gives us examples of His greatness
in creating good out of apparent evil, order out of
apparent chaos and life everlasting after death.

'I have cause today to refer once more to the *Alasotele*

movement and their activities and the effect that these activities have had on us as individuals, as families, as a congregation, and as a town.'

His congregation adjusted themselves in their pews. Some sighed at the recollection of a chapter of their Christian lives which they considered had better be forgotten.

'We have already convinced ourselves that it was the Evil One that was at the bottom of it all and that the true Christian who was familiar with his Bible would have known of the warning about the false Christs and the false prophets who, we are told, will be active in those last days before the real Last Day. We recall today the great tribulation that we as a church have passed through because of the activities of the Evil One and his false prophets – how many members of our congregation were deceived and defected to the *Alasotele* movement. We recall how our church attendances dropped and our church collections practically dried up. But in all our tribulation we put our faith in the Lord Our God, in the knowledge that he would not leave us His children to suffer for ever. And we rejoice that our faith has not been misplaced. For today we have in our midst a good number of our members who have come back for worship and for communion with us in this true house of the Lord.'

A number of people sighed in gratitude to God for the home-coming of the defectors.

'We welcome back our brethren to the true fold of Christ. We do not look upon them as greater sinners than we are. We all, you, and I and they, are miserable sinners. But we are all redeemed in the blood of Christ our Saviour.'

'Allelujah!' One of the newly returned members cried, to the embarrassment of those around him.

'The Lord our God, who specializes in bringing good out of evil and order out of chaos, has in his own inexplicable way chosen the *Alasoteles* as the very instrument of bringing good fortune to our church. My brethren in Christ I have a great announcement to make,' he said, holding up a long envelope. 'I have received a letter from another church called All Souls, in Chicago, in the United States of America. They have sent to us greetings and brotherly love such as should exist between all congregations that believe in the second coming of our Lord. But they have sent more than greetings. They have sent more than brotherly love. They have sent to us an offer of assistance in the building of our new church.'

The congregation were delighted at the information.

'They have read in the newspapers all that happened here in Ibala on 12 August They have read of our church and of our effort to build a new church. They have offered to adopt us and to assist us in our difficulties. They have offered to send to us a first instalment of four thousand dollars. Four thousand dollars,' he repeated. 'That in our own money means one thousand four hundred and seventy-six pounds.'

They all cheered the news. They all went wild with excitement which Rev. Morakinyo thought was perhaps rather unseemly in church.

'Yes, one thousand four hundred and seventy-six pounds,' he continued after the excitement had at last subsided. 'In all, last year, we collected through various functions and from various sources only five hundred and twenty-nine pounds. What our friends from America are giving us now is nearly three times that. And that is not all. They have promised that for every pound that we ourselves collect they will give us another pound. This means that if we collect a hundred pounds at the

Easter thanksgiving service and we send this to the church building fund, then our friends from Chicago in America will send us another hundred pounds.'

Again the congregation cheered the news. The preacher himself was visibly happy. He decided not to chide his hearers for behaving irreverently in the house of the Lord. After the noise had subsided he reminded them of the obligation that the pound-for-pound promise from Chicago placed upon them. Work, real hard work, was necessary and he wound up by emphasizing once more the futility of trying to find reasons for the ways of the Lord and the marvel of his choosing the very *Alasoteles*, who they thought had impaired the progress of their church nearly beyond redemption, as the means of friends stretching to their church the hand of assistance from across the seas.

The Saturday before, Morakinyo had called to see Titus and had given him the information about the church in Chicago adopting the church in Ibala. He had also told him that he had received a letter from Brother Simeon from Bamenda in the Cameroons. From the Chicago church example of good coming out of evil he had propounded to Titus the theory that good would surely come out of the apparent evil of the transfer of Brother Simeon from Ibala to the Cameroons.

On his way to Ibadan the following day Titus pondered the latest developments in Ibala. He wondered why Morakinyo had failed to mention to his congregation the information that the Chicago All Souls had invited him to come to America to preach to their congregation there about the Ibala All Souls and its problems, and about Africa and its people and the spread of the gospel of Christ among them.

He thought that the men of Ibala would have got over their disappointment at not being sucked into the biblical Paradise on 12 August 1950, and gone back to their farms and the women to their cloth-weaving and to the markets if they had been left alone. But they had not been left alone. Their little town had been invaded by newspaper reporters. Naturally it was the local pressmen from Ibadan and Lagos that had arrived on the scene first. But in a matter of days journalists from all over the world had swooped on Ibala. The questions they asked of Bandele, the man who had seen the original vision! And the questions they asked of Titus himself! The episode itself was a great event worthy of publicity and of record. But it was greatly magnified by both the local and the foreign press. Under the screaming headline of '*When Judgement Day came to African Village*' a journalist painted a very lurid account of the events of 12 August and of the people of Ibala. '*Road Maker sees Jesus descending over African Jungle*' another American journal screamed. It published a photograph of Bandele surrounded by six wives and eleven small children. It adorned Bandele with a beard and a halo which the real Bandele did not wear. It showed Bandele's hands outstretched and his face scanning the clouds, obviously in anticipation of their parting to reveal his Lord descending a celestial staircase. Bandele was said to be variously between thirty and sixty and the report made much of the fact that neither he nor anyone living knew his exact age as no vital statistics were kept in the jungles of black Africa. It mentioned the six wives and eleven kids that Bandele kept in the seven huts in his 'kraal' and emphasized the fact that the size of his family was indeed modest, though in keeping with his status in life, as the tribal chief of Ibala had three hundred wives and more children than he himself could count. It mentioned the antelopes and the big snakes which he hunted and the diet of yams and cassava and plantains liberally spiced with pepper on which he lived. It mentioned the trees and rivers and family gods which he worshipped in between visions.

Titus recalled the thesis in the particular article that had been instrumental in bringing the Chicago All Souls in touch with the Ibala Souls. It had been obvious for some time to scholars of theology and of contemporary Christianity, that the Second Coming of the Lord would be through a village in black Africa. This was to demonstrate God's disapproval of racial discrimination.

It was also in appreciation of the fact that the black man was deeply religious and that it must be the Bandeles and the Morakinyos of black Africa that must carry Christian revival back to sinful America and decadent Europe. This particular article made the unfinished church building of All Souls the scene of the events of 12 August instead of Elder Matthew's house, but this enabled them to describe the difficulties that Morakinyo and his congregation were having over their building funds.

Titus pondered the protest articles that were already appearing in the local press and the protest meetings that were already being organized by the nationalists against these lurid articles in the foreign press, which were derogatory to the African. He shook his head at the knowledge that what was meat for Morakinyo and his congregation at All Souls in Ibala was poison for the nationalists at Ibadan and Lagos.

After his official engagement at the office of the Provincial Engineer at Ibadan, Titus drove to the All Races. The club was open from 10 a.m. till midnight but at that time of the day very few people went there.

'You here all the way from Ibala, Mr Oti?' Ian Mc-Lapperton said from the bar. He grinned like an over-grown schoolboy caught playing truant when he should be busy at his lessons. 'Can't stand the blessed heat any longer. Thought I'd drop in to have a beer.'

Titus noticed that with the exception of a couple that spoke in whispers at one corner McLapperton was the only person at the club. 'What will you have, Mr Oti?' he asked as Titus sat on a stool next to him at the bar. Titus asked for a shandy.

'Funny all the things going on in connection with the events of 12 August in Ibala, Mr Oti. An American chap was nearly beaten up here last night. You know, scrounging for news. Went up to Sulaiman's girl, and asked her if she knew how he could get in touch with Bandele and with Simeon. And you know what she told him?' he said, grinning mischievously.

'Tell me.'

'She told him to go to hell, via Soviet Russia.'

They both laughed. The Yard Superintendent went on to say that the way the boys and the girls laughed at the incident was embarrassing and the chairman had to come to the rescue of the foreign journalist.

'Surely he could take a hop to the Cameroons if he was keen on seeing Simeon. I say, how are the boys getting used to his not being around, Ian?'

'Oh, I don't know really. Curiously enough I don't hear people discussing him much. Except the other day in connection with Bimpe.'

'I hear she has disappeared. Gone to join him in the Cameroons, in all probability.'

'That's what the boys say,' McLapperton said after a tender suck at his cigar. 'But, tell me, is it true that both Simeon and Bimpe said the things that everybody's talking about?'

'You mean the confessions? Man, you won't believe it. It was incredible how it all happened.'

'I hear Chris Daniels was there with you and heard it

all too. . . . Now talk of the Devil and doesn't he appear,' McLapperton said, with some excitement as Chris Daniels strolled in.

'Good heavens, Titus,' the lawyer exclaimed. 'Fancy seeing you here now. Titus, I had thought that only the damned like myself and Ian still haunted this den of sin and intemperance, particularly at this time of the day. Would I be contaminating you if I asked you to stand me a beer? I'm broke, flat broke, man. Star if you don't mind. Good old Star. Like Sammy Sparkles says, it's beer at its best.'

After he'd taken a good pull at his drink he put down the glass and sighed. 'Titus, I'm sure whatever designs you had on Bimpe have disappeared with the passing away of the old world on 12 August last. And in this new era after the Coming of Judgement Day to Ibala—'

'A blessing in disguise for Mr Oti, I'm sure. Coast now clear for Bola. I hear she's arriving shortly?'

'In another five days, in fact. One of the reasons I'm here today,' Titus said.

The girl at the corner giggled and all three at the bar turned round to see what was happening. All three pretended not to have seen what they did see as Chris asked for another beer.

'You know something, Chris,' Titus said. 'Ian and I were talking about Simeon Oke and Bimpe as you were coming in.'

'I'm not surprised,' Chris said. 'Everyone does.'

'We haven't really had time to reflect on the fantastic events of 12 August,' Titus said, mischief lighting up his face.

'Quite true, my boy. One thing, I honestly thought that I wouldn't see you ever again this side of Jordan.'

'Go on!'

'Did Simeon Oke really say that he did those things,

Mr Oti? That's what the boys are saying,' Ian McLapperton said, sipping his beer.

'I heard him make the confessions. And what's more Chris here heard him. And Chris was his lawyer. You know what impresses me most in the whole thing? The way the fear of burning for ever in hell-fire made the scoundrel blurt out the truth. Isn't it remarkable that the fellow succeeded in fooling the whole lot of our judicial system – the prosecutor, the defence counsel and the Magistrate. Must be most embarrassing for you as his lawyer,' Titus said, turning to Chris.

After a little silence Chris asked: 'Why do you say that?'

'Why?' Surely he made you believe that he was innocent, didn't he?'

'And who told you that he was not?'

'You must be kidding, Chris,' Titus said seriously. 'You still ask that after his confessions, which you yourself heard with your own ears on 12 August'

Ian McLapperton thought that the lawyer was cornered. 'I suppose that if people won't speak the truth when they are on oath, there's little the courts can do,' he said, coming to the rescue of the lawyer.

Chris charged his glass slowly. 'Just what is truth, my dear roadmaker?' he asked. 'And who told you that what that crank was saying that day was the truth? Surely, even a roadmaker can understand that one does not need to be a medical specialist to know that the fellow was suffering from a brain disease.'

'Chris Daniels,' Titus exclaimed.

'A disease with a long Latin name that I do not expect you to understand. What I expect even you to understand, however, is the very elementary fact that neither the house of Elder Matthew nor its precincts had been properly constituted into a court of law. Neither the old man Matthew nor your Bandele had been sworn in as a Magistrate within the provisions of the Ordinance. Therefore nothing that anyone did or said, nothing that anyone saw or heard when Judgement Day came to Ibala on 12 August last could legally be used in evidence against Simeon Oke, your kinsman, your Foreman.'